Merger Takeover

To Hold

By

Alesanda Elani

Published by Alesanda Elani LLC

Cover design by
AE Designs

E-book ISBN: 978-0-9989124-0-0

Paperback ISBN: 978-0-9989124-1-7

Copyright

Chapter 1: Chris

"Have you heard?" Klaire asked, poking her head through my office door before stepping in.

I turned away from my computer and looked her over. She was beautiful as usual in a red sheath dress and four-inch high heels that complemented her five foot one petite figure. Dark blonde hair hung loose around her shoulders and a light dusting of makeup gave her creamy skin a rosy hue.

"Good afternoon, Klaire. Happy Friday! Please come in and have a seat." I said in mock cheer.

Klaire and I work in the communications department at WingLing Toys, a New York based company that manufactures children's toys. Klaire is the manager of internal communications and I'm the director of social media & public relations.

"We don't have time for pleasantries just now."
She hurried in to take a seat. "*He* is here!" Her voice was hushed.

I leaned back into my chair and raised a brow. "And who, pray tell, is 'He'?"

"Aiden Pierce of Pierce Gaming Enterprises."

"Oh?" I said surprised.

"'Oh' is correct," she said, leaning back in her seat, arms folded and legs crossed.

With the lowest revenues recorded these past few years due to poor management and most recently, a lead poisoning scandal, WingLing Toys had been targeted for a hostile takeover. Or as the story was spun, "a merger" by Pierce Gaming Enterprises, a developer of video games, some of which have been adapted into motion pictures. Aiden Pierce, the company's CEO worked out of their Pittsburgh office and, some years ago, had been infamous for his takeovers, having acquired three toy companies in the span of four years.

Arthur Wing and Jason Ling, the founders of WingLing, fought tooth and nail against the takeover even after nearly putting the company six feet under. Their fight proved unsuccessful when shareholders voted unanimously in favor of new management and forced Wing and Ling into an early retirement within two weeks.

The news of the "merger," however, had left WingLing employees nervous and uncertain of their future with Pierce's arrival, along with a few of his operating team members scheduled for next week. One of the rumors making the rounds was that most of management would be fired and replaced with Pierce's team.

Blinking out of my daze, I brought my attention back to Klaire. "I thought he was due to arrive next Thursday."

"Yeah, you and the whole office thought that. I heard he is unpredictable and works his employees to the bone. I wonder if they meant that in a sexual way because he is *hottt*!"

"Seriously? Are you 12?" I asked.

"Well, he is good-looking even with the permanent scowl etched into his features."

"You've met him?"

"No, but I did some googling and let me tell you," she whispered, leaning closer, which had me unconsciously doing the same. "He looks like a Greek god! A wall of muscles I would not mind climbing. A mountain peak I could sit on. Abs I would gladly lick. Arms so strong, I could –"

"Klaire Michaels!" I shouted. "Snap out of it."

For the past five months, Wing, Ling, myself, and two others from the comms department had been working covertly with the PGE team, corresponding only via phone, email, and secret video conferences, to structure a unified narrative for the public – one that reflected WingLing's new mission and goals. Social media messages, press releases and new content for the websites were drafted to uniformly align with PGE's commitment to its shareholders, employees, and communities. All of these were to be released following an internal staff meeting informing the employees of the changes.

All communications I'd had with Aiden Pierce were strictly via email. I would send him strategy recommendations and draft statements, and he in turn would veto some of the recommendations and have endless revisions until I was about ready to fling myself out a window.

I cleared my throat. "Don't you have work to do today? And how would you know about the contours of his abdominal muscles?"

"Hellooo, *Google*. I could tell from the way his shirts fit. You know I have an eye for these things," she continued, "It looks like he'll be working out of our office."

"What! Why?" This was definitely news to me.

"Apparently, he 'wants to keep a finger on the pulse of the challenges facing WingLing'. And what a long thick finger it is."

I stifled a laugh. "You got that from a few online images? You need help!"

Feeling guilty for not being able to tell her about the covert team working with PGE and my email exchanges with Mr. Pierce due to confidentiality, I tried to change the subject.

"And what does Markus think of you lusting after our soon-to-be new boss?" I asked, referring to her live-in boyfriend of one-plus years.

She threw her hands up unrepentantly. "I'm 29, not dead. I can appreciate another beautiful man and I assure you, Markus loves my lusty ways."

I laughed and turned back to my computer, scanning my Outlook for any urgent emails and hoping she would take the hint. I loved Klaire to pieces, but when she visited my office we'd end up chatting for way too long and then I ended up staying until 9 p.m. playing catch up.

"And while we're on the subject, when are *you* going to get back in the swing of things?"

"The swing of what things?" I asked, not looking away from my monitor.

"The swing of dating, sexing a hot boy or man, and please don't give me the 'I'm focusing on my career' BS. No one is that busy. Honey, you need to get laid." She admonished.

"Please don't turn into my mother right now, and I was laid not too long ago." I half lied, hoping she'd lay off, but of course I knew better.

I turned to find her eying me suspiciously. "Really? When? By who? By what?"

"You think I tell you everything? And did you just ask *by what*?"

"I was just trying to make a point," she grinned. "So, who laid you? No, your vibrator does not count!"

"Well, remember the guy from that uppity lounge a couple weeks back?"

"The one with the name I hated?"

I smiled. "Yes. Olivor."

"The one I told you to run away from?"

"Yes. The very same."

"What the fuck kind of name is Olivor anyway"?

I leaned back in my chair exasperated. "Do you want to hear this or not?"

"Yes, please continue."

"Well, after days of texting, mostly from him, I decided, why not? So, we met up for happy hour at Salsa Carne Grill."

"Oh yum, best and strongest margaritas on the planet." She sighed.

"Focus," I said, impatiently. "After a few drinks, we went back to his place. We made-out, he fondled my boobs, he fingered me to *non*-completion, I gave him a couple tugs, he came, then we fell asleep."

Klaire stared at me like a deer in headlights. "And what happened *next*?"

"Nothing. I woke up the next morning and snuck out."

Her jaw dropped. "And at what point were you getting laid?"

Fluttering my lashes and pouting innocently I said, "Did you miss the part where we fell asleep? Technically, we did *lay* together."

She glared at me. "Firstly, you *lie* in a bed and *lay* a book down so there was no *laying* of any kind going on."

I busted out laughing. "Touché."

"Secondly, did you get your Master's in public relations & corporate communications only to go back to high school? Because all of that drivel," she paused, gesturing with her hands, "is some high school BS!"

"You're ri –"

She cut me off with a raised hand. "Thirdly," she said shaking her head. "You're sad you know that?"

I nodded. "Yes."

"And not only are you sad, but you make me sad too."

I looked down, guiltily.

"And lastly, did you say 'touché'? You hate that word and wish it banned from use. Or did you think you could just slip it in while I was distracted during my tirade?"

I laughed, "I'm sorry, I shouldn't have said it, I couldn't find a better word to express myself."

"Christen James, I love you, but you seriously need to relax and let a hot sexy piece of man beef poke you a few times. Act like the young and restless 28-year-old that you are, not a timid teenager or old maid."

"Restless?" I asked.

"It sounded complimentary in my head."

"Thanks. I'll set a calendar reminder for that."

"You have a banging bod, naturally tanned and glowing skin, abs I would push my sister under a moving bus for, a luscious ass, and your best feature of all…those perky D-cup titties. You deserve a man who will appreciate and take care of them."

I stared at her, speechless. "Four things, Klaire Michaels." Counting down with my fingers, I began, "One, 'naturally tanned and glowing skin'? Seriously? Do you write for skin commercials in your spare time? Two, don't say the word 'titties' ever again. I mean *ever*. Three, how long have you been in love with me? I'm extremely flattered. And four, I need a man to take care of *them*? But not me as a whole?"

She shrugged. "Well they are pretty spectacular. Remember that one time –"

"At band camp?" I interrupted.

"Don't be cute." She grinned. "That one time we went lingerie shopping and I accidently copped a feel?" She used air quotes on the word "accidentally." "They were so firm and perky. I *almost* felt bad for thinking they were fake when we first met."

"Why did you *almost* feel bad?"

"Well, because I thought you were brilliant and beautiful, but you were kinda bitchy to me at first. I was hoping you didn't have absolutely everything going for you."

I rolled my eyes.

"Your boobies are pretty spectacular," I said. "Wait, why are we still discussing boobs?"

She shrugged, then cupped her breasts. "Yeah, nice C cups I guess, but they could be bigger."

"Your head could be bigger. Please get out of my office." I turned back to my inbox.

"By the way, a managers' meeting with The Executioner is being scheduled for Monday." Klaire said as she shoved her chair back.

My gaze met hers. "What?"

She stood, removing invisible lint from her sweater dress. "Aiden Pierce. Monday. 8 a.m. We're all getting fired."

"Why didn't you tell me this before? And how do you know this and I don't?"

Klaire strode towards the door before turning back to face me. "That's what I came in here to tell you, but we got sidetracked."

Straightening my back, I placed both hands on my waist. "*You* got sidetracked."

"Same difference," she dismissed. "I saw a team of people moving boxes into the offices on the top floor so I followed, to snoop."

Confused, I asked "What about Wing and Ling? They still have two weeks left."

"I know. The office is abuzz with this new development. I'm told they'll be working the rest of their time from home, but coming in to attend meetings."

Taking a few steps closer, she said, "I also ran into Lucas Hunt, Mr. Pierce's Head of Operations. He introduced himself and asked for my title and department, then took a call on his cell and walked away. Completely dismissing me *before* I even finished responding!! I mean how rude! He thinks he can treat people like that just because he's easy on the eyes?" she barked.

"You ran into him where?"

"I mean why ask a question if you don't want an answer?" she continued rhetorically.

"I'm still waiting for an answer to my question," I interrupted.

She huffed. "Now I'm all worked up again. I forgot how angry I was when I came in here."

"Well?" I prompted.

"On the 20th floor when I was snooping. Hellooo, weren't you listening?"

"And there's a managers' meeting on Monday?"

"Yeesss." She slowly nodded her head back and forth as if talking to a moron.

Interesting, I thought.

"When I got up there, Melvin was cleaning out Mr. Wing's office. I asked what's up and he said Mr. Pierce had requested a file on all employees in the office and would be scheduling meetings with the department managers." Klaire made her way towards my office door. "We're still going out tonight right?"

"I might be here late," I replied.

"It's Friday, don't be a loser!"

And with that she was gone, leaving me with my thoughts.

Chapter 2: Chris

Monday morning arrived a lot sooner than I would have liked, per usual. I barely had a chance to relax this weekend with my three brothers all showing up for dinner at my parents' house in Brooklyn Sunday night, which they normally found all sorts of crazy excuses to avoid. Being the youngest and the only girl, they never missed an opportunity to mercilessly tease me. Usually, it was 'Why are you so skinny?' – I'm five foot six and about 130 pounds – or asking questions about what guy I was dating so they could kick his ass, as if I was still in high school, to pleading with me to come back and work for them at one of their gyms. This teasing, however, was a big improvement from my childhood of disfiguring my dolls, leaving worms on my dresser and making me play their outdoor shooting games where I was always the enemy target to be pelted with plastic bullets. They were super assholes.

Two of my brothers; David and Daniel, had started a boxing gym in New Jersey eight years ago, which became a big success. They now owned and operated three full-service fitness centers called BoxFlex

Fitness. The original and now remodeled gym was located in New Jersey while the other two were in New York and Connecticut. I started my career in communications as the media and public relations specialist for BoxFlex during my senior year of college. I left after four years to complete my Master's at NYU and later accepted a position at WingLing Toys. Matthew, the youngest of my brothers, decided to go down a different path and is a lawyer living in Chicago, but made occasional trips to the city.

Saturday night hadn't been relaxing either. Klaire had forced me to join her and Markus for cocktails at a new restaurant in lower Manhattan. With one restaurant always closing up shop and others popping up all around the city, there was never a lack for new places to try. This was one of the many things I loved about the city I grew up in.

Walking through the automatic glass sliding doors of the WingLing building, I gave a quick wave to the security desk and made my way to the elevators. The building had 20 floors with WingLing occupying the top three, and boasted an open rooftop that was perfect for ogling Manhattan's skyline not to mention getting away for a few moments of peace and alone time. The rooftop was restricted to upper level staff members and could only be accessed through the company's keycard, except when in use for a party or special event.

To start off my daily work week routine, I made a quick stop at my office to drop off my things and refill my water bottle in the kitchen, then headed to the gym on the bottom level for a 45-minute run on the treadmill.

Chapter 3: Aiden

THIS MACHINE IS SHIT! Not surprising since the lat pulldown wasn't any better. I completed my last set of reps on the bench press and started on the pullup bar facing the wall when I heard the gym door open and slam shut. My much needed solitude was up. Although, when I came in at 5:30 a.m. this morning, I was pleasantly surprised to find an empty workout room, especially in a city where almost everyone I knew hit the gym at the crack of dawn.

It felt good to be back in the city permanently, even under the circumstances, but I wished I had returned sooner. Making the decision to attend college in California had been an impulsive one. At the time, I wanted nothing more than to escape to a state as far away from my father as possible, the man who caused the deaths of my mother and little brother. Being absent two years ago, when my mother passed away, was something I would always regret. Then again, it was just another item to add to my long list of regrets. The hatred I had felt for my father and towards myself drove me to flee the city 16 years ago. The launch of my company kept me away and my selfishness prevented me from being there for my mother when she needed me most.

Instead, I was too preoccupied with creating my first marketable line of video games with Keaton Javies, a close friend from Berkeley. Keaton worked on form and aesthetics, making sure the handheld games were comfortable enough to be held for long periods of time in addition to being visually pleasing. Keaton was now in charge of all manufacturing and product development in Pittsburgh, the city we decided was the most cost-effective location for a manufacturing plant. We relocated there shortly after graduation.

Completing the last of my chest and back workout routines, I turned to do some crunches when I was halted in my tracks.

Fuck.

There was a woman running on the treadmill, in the tiniest shorts I'd ever seen, with an ass that was more than enough to fill my hands and just high enough to balance a shot of whiskey.

Lowering my eyes, I took in the small gap created by a pair of smooth, curvy legs. I suddenly noticed that the legs and ass were no longer in motion. Lifting my gaze further up, I saw that the ass belonged to a gorgeous woman with a set of caramel eyes that were currently shooting daggers at me through the wall-mounted mirrors. I crossed my arms and gave her a sardonic grin, daring her to say something.

She pressed a button on the treadmill, grabbed a water bottle, and stepped off. I waited anxiously as she turned around to face me, while I used the opportunity to take in the rest of her: dark-brown wavy hair piled high on her head in a nest of sorts, large breasts that looked firm and ripe – *real?* I wondered – were encased in a blue sports bra that was visible through a dark pink long-sleeved top, narrow waist, and of course, the *inappropriate* shorts that revealed more ass than they covered and the reason I had now missed two minutes of valuable workout time.

Did she just huff?

"Are you done gawking?" She asked.

My gaze fell to pouty lips that begged to be bitten, and I took a small step closer. "You do realize this is a corporate building, don't you? And those shorts are inappropriate to say the least." Everything about her body was inappropriate and made me harder with every passing minute.

Her face reddened in what I suspected was embarrassment. "I don't normally wear these, I did laundry over the weekend and packed the wrong bottoms–" she was saying and abruptly stopped as if wondering why she'd bothered with an explanation.

Not the response I was expecting.

Her chestnut eyes showed a flash of sincerity then turned angry. "And if you have a problem with them you could look away, not *leer* at me like a pervert!" she snapped. "Are you the building police?"

I took two more steps forward until my chest was nearly touching her face. She stood her ground, but the look on her face said she despised having to pull her head back to see my face.

I crouched down to look into big mocha colored eyes. "If I were the police I would arrest you for indecent ass exposure and lewd conduct." She was breathing harder now and I paused for effect, her heaving chest drawing my eyes to her luscious tits. "And while you were handcuffed in the back of my car, I'd show you just how much of a pervert I can be."

Shock briefly crossed her impassive expression. "Is that supposed to shock me?"

I gave her a slow smile, took her hand, and brought it to my cock. "If it's shock you want, I'm more than happy to oblige."

At the loud sound of the door opening, she jolted and scrambled away. "Wait," I called after her.

"Wait." I repeated, feeling more than irritated as she headed straight for the door.

"Good morning, Mr. Pierce," said the male intruder.

I ignored him and watched as her hand briefly paused on the door handle before she ran out.

Fuck! I didn't even get a name.

"How was your weekend?" the intruder continued.

I scowled at him.

CHAPTER 4: CHRIS

"OH SHIT! OH SHIT! OH SHIT!" I chanted as I headed for the ladies' locker room to shower.

Was that Aiden Pierce? I admit, I did google him, but he looked nothing like the photos online. The real-life

Pierce was taller, broader and bigger. He was half man, half panther with longish jet-black tousled hair that curled slightly behind his ears. A full beard with faded side burns that highlighted the chiseled angles of his face and drew me into pools of midnight blue eyes. Eyes that were knowing and all consuming. Eyes that had me confessing crimes I'd only thought about committing.

There had been numerous articles that included photos of his Pittsburgh facility and video game lines and a few with gorgeous exotic women at galas and corporate events. However, none of the articles disclosed any personal information besides his birthday, and if accurate, he would be turning 34 years old five months from now.

Game plan strategy: Avoid him by any means necessary.

After I showered, I dressed in a green knee-length fitted pencil skirt, navy dress shirt with sleeves rolled up to my elbows, and my go-to navy suede four-inch Anouk Jimmy Choo pumps. I left the gym and took the elevators up to my office. I needed coffee, stat!

"How was your workout?" Klaire's voiced drifted into the kitchen while I waited for the Nespresso machine to finish my brew.

I turned and eyed her suspiciously, trying not to give anything away. "Umm…. why do you ask? What have you heard?"

She walked past me to place a Tupperware in the fridge. "Umm…. why are you being weird? Didn't you work out this morning?

"Right. Yes. It was good." I picked up my coffee and made a beeline for my office with Klaire close on my heels. I sat behind my desk and sipped my coffee while my computer booted up. "So, what room is the 8 o'clock meeting in again?" I asked, already knowing the answer, but wanting to distract her. A ploy that rarely worked.

She leaned against the chair across from me, looking contemplative before shaking her head. "The Tesla Room."

The Tesla Room was one of six conference rooms named as a result of Arthur Wing and Jason Ling's fondness for sports cars. The Tesla room was one of the largest with seating for over 30 people. It was also located on the 20th floor, Pierce's floor and the very floor I needed to avoid for as long as reasonably possible, especially after our gym encounter.

Klaire took a seat, her eyes glued to her phone. "I thought the meeting would be taking place on our floor with all the renovations and whatnot going on the 20th floor, but then Margaret changed the Outlook invite location from TBD to Tesla Room Sunday night."

"Yeah, I saw that. Who's Margaret anyway? And what renovations are you talking about"?

"Mr. Pierce requested some changes to his office and wants the tiles in his bathroom replaced with marble. And Margaret or Marge, as she prefers to be called, is his assistant."

I tried to laugh and nearly choked on my coffee. "What kind of tiles were in there before?" What an arrogant, high maintenance ass.

"Hell, if I know."

I shook my head in amazement. "How do you know these things?"

"I work internal comms. I know it all." She stood and motioned for me to follow. "Let's go. Meeting starts in 20 and I'd prefer to be sitting, not standing."

"I hardly think you need 20 minutes to secure a seat."

"Yes. We do. It's the first meeting with the new boss and no one wants to be late."

I squirmed a little. "I've got a lot to catch up on. How about you fill me in afterwards."

"What the fuck is going on?" She asked, giving me her don't'-fuck-with-me look.

I squirmed some more before answering, firing rapidly. "There was an incident in the gym this morning. I really don't want to talk about it now and besides *you'll* be late for the meeting. I plan to avoid him for as long as I can get away with it. Starting with this meeting."

Her voice was calm when she said, "Ok, I assume this incident involves Mr. Pierce? And you're right, we can't talk about it now because *we're* going to be late. No, you can't miss this meeting. It's probably going to run over the one hour allotted time frame and surely you can't expect me to relay everything discussed."

I slumped down in my chair.

"The room won't seat all 70 employees so we can just hide behind the folks standing in the back." She continued at my defeated look. "Besides, if you were your usual sweaty, unkempt mess during your workout, I doubt he'll recognize you."

I glowered at her.

"You transform quite nicely." She smiled.

"There are 56 employees in this building not 70." I challenged unnecessarily.

"Tomayto, tomaato. I was rounding up. Come on sweetcheeks, let's go."

Six minutes later, behind the standing crowd, we hid.

After a few introductory and somewhat reassuring comments, Pierce pointed out the benefits of the 'merger,' what we could hope to expect in the upcoming months and foreseeable future and touched briefly on a few changes to our business-as-usual routine. He further went on to discuss new initiatives and goals, the economic environment, and our financial trajectory.

As he continued in a deep gravelly sex-coma-inducing voice that vied for your attention and won, his midnight eyes – looking much lighter now – scanned the room. I held my breath and slumped low in my standing position, relaxing only when he moved aside and faced away from my direction as Lucas Hunt, VP of operations, began his spiel.

The meeting ran well over an hour and came to a close with Pierce expressing his appreciation for Wing and Ling's "continued cooperation during the transition," and leaving us with a final statement that we weren't sure was meant to reassure us or have us packing up our work stations.

"...in these highly competitive times and despite the appearance of our unexpected profit growth, let us strive to do better than our best so that anything less does not become the disappearance of our standing with Pierce Gaming Enterprises. Marge, my EA, will send meeting notices to all department heads and managers to take place in the next couple of weeks."

And with that, Pierce exited the room. The rest of us followed suit shortly after, with a few exchanging worried glances.

Chapter 5: Aiden

Standing behind my office desk, I took in a sea of endless skyscrapers, a view made even more absolute through the floor-to-ceiling windows.

"It's fucking good to be back," I said to Lucas who was sprawled comfortably in one of the new pieces of furniture my office had been remodeled with over the weekend.

"I recall your words being, '*The traffic is a fucking nightmare,*'" he said.

"It is."

"Have you seen your father since you've been back?"

At the abrupt change in subject, I turned back to face Lucas and took a seat behind the mahogany desk

"No," I replied.

Thanks to some news outlets, my father was made aware of my move back to New York after 15 years. Ever since, I'd received nonstop calls from him and his latest girlfriend, whom I had only met twice before. I didn't necessarily hate my father; I just wanted nothing to do with him.

"The office looks good. The contractors worked quickly enough," Lucas said, changing the subject.

Lucas and I have been friends for over nine years, and having been privy to my life's story, he knew when to drop the subject of Isaac Pierce.

I nodded. "Yes, I'm very pleased."

Over the weekend, several very well-paid contractors worked tirelessly to turn my previous office into one I would work in. The wall separating the smaller office next door had been knocked down to increase the floor space. The carpeting and flooring were redone, the adjoining private bathroom remodeled with marble tiles, and all previous furniture replaced. The end result was a decent 650 square foot suite that included: a six-seat conference table, a wood-paneled bookshelf, and a glass display of video games developed by PGE. And off to one corner was a seating area with a flat screen TV and game console display.

I pressed the speaker button on the office phone and dialed my assistant.

"Yes, Mr. Pierce?" Marge answered.

"Who do we have left?"

"Chris James. He's your last meeting for the day."

"Didn't we have him on the calendar last week?"

"Yes, twice actually. The first time we had to reschedule due to a conflict on his end and the second time I had to cancel to accommodate your apartment viewing."

"Right. What time is that for?"

"5 o'clock, so in about 13 minutes."

"Thanks Marge." I ended the call.

"I'm actually looking forward to meeting him. The press release he sent out during the WingLing lead scandal was pretty impressive," Lucas said, perusing through some files, an ankle crossed over his knee.

"You can say that again, not to mention the balls it took."

CHAPTER 6: CHRIS

"OH GOD, I AM SO NOT READY FOR THIS," I said to my reflection in the bathroom mirror. My dark brown hair fell in loose waves down my back as I touched up my lightly applied makeup with one last stroke of mascara and barely-there matted lipstick. I took a few deep breaths, smoothing down my beige satin short-sleeved top and dark red pencil skirt, and walked my navy suede-covered pumps out of the bathroom.

Stepping out of the elevator on the 20th floor, I walked down the short hallway towards Wing and Ling's former offices and through glass double doors. I came to a stop in front of a desk where a woman who looked to be in her fifties was seated with glasses halfway down her nose.

"Hello. Marge?" I asked.

"Yes," she said, pulling her glasses away from her face.

"I'm here for my 5 o'clock with Mr. Pierce and Mr. Hunt."

She gave me an odd look, a bewildered expression taking over her smooth features. "You're Christopher James?"

Christopher? Where had she gotten that from? "I'm Christen James." I said.

"Oh! I'm sorry."

Glancing at the wall clock above her head I asked, "May I go in now?"

"Yes, of course, Mr. Pierce's office is just around the corner."

I proceeded in her pointed direction. "Thanks."

I came to a stop at the only closed door around the corner and knocked. Without awaiting a response, I turned the handle and stepped in.

The office was quite the transformation. I almost wowed out loud. It was spacious and stunning, completely reimagined from its previous state. I took several steps towards a large hardwood desk where Pierce was seated, and across from him was Lucas Hunt.

"Hello, Mr. Hunt, Mr. Pierce," I said, and was met with complete silence. "May I take a seat?"

There was no response.

I pulled out the empty chair next to Hunt and sat down.

"And you are?" Lucas asked, shifting into an upright position. His intense yet neutral expression highlighted the severe angles that made up his exquisite features. His dark brown hair was stylized in a disconnected pompadour with faded sides and a top that defied gravity.

"Chris. Your 5 o'clock," I said to Hunt, and turned to face Pierce who was staring at me with consuming eyes. His beard was much shorter than the last time I'd seen him and he wore that sexy 5 o'clock shadow like it was his right.

"You're late," Pierce stated, his gaze dropping to my chest and holding for a couple seconds as if wondering where he's seen it, or *them* before.

I tried to appear unaffected, but my skin felt as if it were on a stovetop set to medium heat. "Yes. Sorry about that. Shall we begin?"

"What's your full *first* name?" Lucas asked.

Christopher apparently. "Christen, with a C."

"Nice name," he said.

"Thank you."

"Pardon our earlier confusion. We didn't know you were a woman," Hunt said clearing his throat. "A female." He corrected.

"It's a bit sexist of you to assume I was a male, don't you think?" I teased, glancing briefly at Pierce. He stared back with eyes that looked icy and smoldering at the same time, yet he didn't utter a word. His crisp white dress shirt fit him in a way that made me thirsty. The rolled-up sleeves revealed strong arms dusted with dark hairs. For no reason at all, I imagined grabbing onto them and holding on for dear life. Klaire was right, his body was like a ladder I would so love to climb.

Lucas's expression remained stoic. They were like Mr. Serious and Mr. Super Serious. "We wanted to meet with each of the department managers so we could be briefed on what each team has in their pipeline and discuss any existing or potential issues."

Since Lucas was the only one speaking, I turned to him and gave him my full attention. I went through a list of the press and media communications my team and I had set for release, along with timelines and updates to the websites and social media messaging and graphics.

"That's great," Hunt said, and sounded genuinely impressed. "I know you worked with Aiden and other members of our team a few months prior to our arrival on content and language, so we're up to speed on that front. Thanks again for your discretion regarding those matters."

"Sure, you're welcome," I said.

"I would like to discuss the lead poisoning incident." Pierce interjected.

I was momentarily taken aback by the abrupt change in subject. I shifted slowly in my chair to face him. "Ok."

"How were you not fired after the stunt you pulled?" he asked, his lips barely moving and eyes appearing glacial.

About a year ago, the latest line of toys manufactured by WingLing from their Voltrox series was released in stores nationwide. During the first four months on shelves, there were two reported incidents of lead poisoning involving children who had recently come into contact with toys from the Voltrox line. When the toys were tested, results showed infinitesimal traces of lead. And upon receiving the results of the testing, WingLing opted to not only leave the toys on shelves, but they continued production.

When a third case was reported, I immediately drafted a press statement stating that WingLing would be issuing a nationwide recall of the entire Voltrox line and halting all of its production. WingLing rejected my assertion of a recall – an assertion that was also shared by most department heads as a no brainer – preferring to wait and see how things played out. Strongly disagreeing with a decision that I found not only morally reprehensible, but against all rules of corporate responsibility, I went against WingLing and released the recall statement to the press. This in turn forced WingLing to pull the Voltrox line off shelves.

At the time, I knew I was putting my job at risk, but it was worth it to me. And the recall ended up saving the company from potential lawsuits. However, WingLing's delayed reaction to the crisis negatively impacted its stocks and was one of the many reasons the board had voted in favor of new management.

Fuming on the inside, I took a breath to calm myself and plastered on a smile that said, *If you thought I was in the wrong, then you could go take a bleeping leap off a short pier.* "I kept my job because that *stunt* was the best and only option for everyone involved." Leaning forward, I continued. "I don't regret my decision and I would gladly do it all over again." Surely, he didn't disagree with that.

"I don't disagree." Pierce said.

Not taking shit from people was something I sometimes exceled at, so if he wants to be an ass about this, I say bring it on. Glacially darkening eyes and all.

Hold up. Wait a minute. Stop! Did he just say he *doesn't* disagree?

Okay, so why were we having this conversation? *And of course*, he doesn't disagree. What kind of person would?

There was a moment of silence.

CHAPTER 7: AIDEN

CHRIST! SHE WAS FUCKING BEAUTIFUL. Exotically stunning. My little gym bunny. Her stubborn pouty lips were begging to be kissed, licked, pulled, bitten, sucked, and fucked. Watching her for the past 30 minutes, all I could think of were the ways I wanted to take her. The ways I *will* take her.

I didn't know why I was looking to start a fight. Maybe I wanted to punish her for her misleading name. After numerous email exchanges during these past five months, it never occurred to me that *Chris* was in fact a female. Not that it would have made a difference in our interaction, but it would have been nice to not have been caught off guard. Or maybe I wanted to punish her because for the past eight days since our gym encounter, I had come in my shower while I pictured fucking her and coming all over her perfect ass. Maybe it was the fact that her intelligence, standing up to what she believed in, and especially her stubborn mouth, had gotten me so hard. It was taking all I had to not lunge for her and force her to submit to my will. Even having had more than my share of women, I couldn't recall ever feeling this strongly about wanting another or *needing* one beneath me. So no, I didn't feel the least bit guilty about picking a fight.

I reclined into my leather chair and casually studied the nuance of each expression that fleetingly crossed her face. "Do you have a problem with authority?" I asked.

Lucas swung a *back-the-fuck-off* look in my direction. A look I disregarded without hesitation. The small crack in her beautiful smile belied the simmering anger I knew she felt, and I also knew that if she could have her way at this moment, I would be toppling over on the floor from a swift kick to the groin. The thought almost had me smiling. However, she kept her composure, and I admired that about her. I admired most everything about her.

There was a slight pursing of her lips before she said, "I'm going to need you to elaborate."

"I'm sure we can all agree that the recall was absolutely necessary, but do you think the way you handled it was determinative of the solution?"

I caught the puzzled look that she immediately schooled. "How would you have handled it differently?"

"I'm the one asking the questions." My clipped voice sounded harsher than I had intended, but the sly smile that curved her distracting lips, made me feel less of a jerk.

"I don't believe I have a problem with authority, however, if this authority were morally irresponsible, or say, being a bully and abusing *his* or her power," she shrugged, "who's to say what I might do."

Lucas cleared his throat, breaking the staring standoff which had ensued. "It looks like our time is–"

51

he was saying when Christen abruptly stood and I interrupted.

"Lucas, please give us a minute?" My eyes were still fixed on her.

"Sure." Lucas said, attempting to get my attention with a warning look as he walked out of the office.

I ignored him.

"Christen! Sit!" I ordered and stood to walk around my desk. Leaning against it, I folded my arms and arched a brow as I waited for her to comply.

"I asked you to sit." I said in a low voice.

She took a nervous step backwards which made me want to reach for her and pull her to me. "You *commanded* me to sit."

"I guess you do have a problem with authority," I said, and wasn't sure if the comment kindled her anger, but I did notice the way her breathing had changed, which drew my gaze to her heaving chest, and suddenly all I wanted was to see beneath her blouse.

"Are you going to arrest me?" she taunted on a whisper.

"Do you want me to?" I volleyed back.

Slowly, I raked my gaze down her body and back to the voluptuous swell of breasts that reminded me of a bountiful harvest after a cruel famine. "Nice to see you in more appropriate clothing," I lied. It would be nice to see her in absolutely nothing.

I got no response.

I needed to put a stop to this before I said and did something even more unprofessional than I already had. I took a deep breath and briefly closed my eyes, but instead of getting a clearer head, I got a subtle whiff of her scent. Warm vanilla and wet sex.

Christ!

I shook my head to force a mental reset back to network settings and again moved around the desk to mold myself into the awaiting leather chair. "Do I need to worry about you going rogue if I gave a directive you disagree with?"

"No," She stated firmly.

"Alright. That will be all."

Chapter 8: Chris

It had been over two weeks since my meeting with Pierce and Hunt and also the last time I had seen either one. Pierce's frequent trips to Pittsburgh and other work-related travel kept him away from the office as much as when he was in. Our correspondence, which had been restricted to emails prior to his arrival, now included phone calls and on occasion, text messages. He was often a rude condescending asshole, but little did he know that I had two assholes for brothers and one of the benefits was learning to toughen up at an early age. And although I was accustomed to the fine art of assholery, his brand often threw me for a loop. He would quietly hang up the phone close to the end of a meeting while I was still speaking, only to later realize I'd been talking to myself for the past eight minutes. His emails weren't any better; I would send several paragraphs, only to receive two worded responses such as; 'redo it," 'rephrase please!' and 'needs work,' all without specifying which parts he took issue with.

Luckily for me, his absences meant I didn't have to work so hard at avoiding him which also meant most days I could sometimes resume my morning workout schedule rather than having to wait until the end of the work day. But most importantly, I didn't have to be faced with the panty-melting attraction I felt for him, assholery and all. And I knew he was attracted to me as well, if the smoldering and intense looks during our meeting were anything to go by. Then again, all his looks were intense, so maybe that wasn't saying much.

I wrapped up the last of my meetings for the afternoon and made a quick trip to the kitchen to grab a smoothie. One of the changes that had come from the merger was a complete remolding of the office kitchens, which now included a cappuccino machine and smoothie maker. I was very grateful for the latter. I sampled my delicious strawberry banana concoction and strolled over to Klaire's office for a quick chat. I knocked on the door, and entered upon hearing a groan that made me laugh.

"Hey you!" I said, stepping in and plopping myself into the chair across from her.

"Don't, 'hey you,' me!" she snapped with a contemptuous look.

"I would ask what's got your thong in a twist, but I know you don't wear any?" I teased.

Her emerald eyes narrowed daggers at me. "Your little *covert comms committee*, that's what!"

Uh oh!

How the hell had she found out? I had felt guilty and about the secrecy, but didn't think it was that big of a deal. It was my job to *not* disclose any information until the merger/takeover was complete.

"Honey, I was sworn to secrecy. Please don't be upset," I begged.

"It's not the fact that you kept the details secret per se. It's the fact that you keep *a* secret from me, period. And about my own freaking department."

I sat up straighter in my chair, my expression sincere and pleading.

"Ok, maybe I am mad about the whole thing!" she said.

"Babe, I'm sorry," I said with an exaggerated sad face.

For a moment she simply stared back at me.

"Ok, but I don't want to talk to you right now. I need some time to try and see things more rationally."

Her sad expression weighed down on my chest. "How did you find out?"

"I'm not telling you because like I said, I'm not talking to you right now."

I bet it was Liz who also worked in internal comms with Klaire and who also happened to be on the committee. That woman couldn't keep a secret to save her life. Especially when it came to other people's secrets.

I nodded. "I can accept that, but we have the bi-weekly comms update meeting next Wednesday so we have to talk soon, not to mention all the other things we work on together."

"I'm aware, which is why I intend to only speak to you in a work-related capacity."

She sounded bratty and from her upturned chin, she knew it, but she meant every word. I could say she was being overly dramatic, but Klaire was one of the most loyal people I knew and she didn't take kindly to dishonesty.

"Ok. Let me know when you're ready to talk." I stood and walked towards her door. "I'm sorry," I said, and exited her office.

Chapter 9: Aiden

Being back in the office was something I had looked forward to all week, despite the video conferences, calls, and meetings that never ceased even when I was away. I looked forward to seeing Christen's beautiful face and even missed her stubborn mouth. I hadn't been able to get thoughts of her out of my head, and almost felt bad for making her doubt the great work she did, with my dismissive remarks and short responses during our phone calls and email exchanges. I resented the effect she had on me, especially since I *never* mixed business with pleasure. An effect that hadn't diminished even after my last fuck with Petra. Petra was someone who managed a restaurant I frequented and who I was also seeing casually in Pittsburgh for the past two months. In my line of work, I rarely worked directly with women and never had the urge to sleep with one. What I felt for Christen wasn't just about sex. I found her work to be impressive and on some level admired her fervid stance on right and wrong. She was tenacious and steadfast. And I wanted to corrupt her.

I'd been traveling for a couple of weeks with most of my time spent in Pittsburgh, completing the transition to New York and packing up the rest of my property. My realtor had my apartment listed for sale, and after six apartment viewings in New York, I finally purchased one I could call home. A two-level, four-bedroom, four and a half bath, 5,800 square foot penthouse, located on the 78th floor set atop one of Manhattan's tallest skyscrapers and boasting a panoramic view of the city. The furnished apartment, most of which I had emptied so I could redecorate to suit my tastes, now sat empty save for the Arata-styled California king bed in the master bedroom.

Since my return, I had visited my mom and brother's grave sites, something I always did whenever I was in the city. During my visits, I would tell them about the newest games I had in development and how sorry I was for not doing more for Ian after his injury, and for my absence when Mom needed me most.

I wondered if the ache I felt inside would ever subside or if it would always be a part of me. The memories of the short precious years I had with Ian were still so vivid, and I hoped to never forget. His love of sports and fondness for video games were things we had shared, and we dreamt of starting our own company someday. I wanted to design games that worked on every platform, and he wanted games that allowed users to make their own mods as well as a handheld console discreet enough to get away with playing in class. The thought always brought a smile to my face. In high school, I played basketball while Ian played soccer his first and only year of high school. Sixteen years later, I had the company we dreamt of starting together, and he was not standing with me.

After weeks of sending my father's calls to voicemail, I relented and agreed to a lunch meeting with him, if for no other reason than to get the calls to stop.

I spent the rest of my day back in the office in the game room with Lucas, testing out new interfaces and prototypes while internally scheming up ways to get some alone time with Christen. With her being in media and public relations, there wasn't a need for us to interact on a daily basis. It was about 7:30pm when I left the game room to head out for the evening, having decided to simply stop by her office in the morning.

Chapter 10: Chris

A day later and still getting the silent treatment from Klaire, I wrote a silly poem and sent it to her.

Roses are red, violets are blue

I miss your green gaze and now in a haze

without you

Come back to me Klaire, I think the world of

you

Two hours later and not a word from her.

And on a downer note, Pierce was back in the office. Just knowing only a floor separated us made my heart race well into the evening. I was so busy all afternoon and hadn't realized how quiet and late it had gotten. I retrieved some bills from my wallet. Stuffing them into the pocket of my yellow pencil skirt, I pushed away from my computer and headed to the elevator. The vending machines on the lower levels had the best junk food. I strolled through the nearly empty office to reach the bank of elevators and pressed the call button. When one of the doors opened, without paying attention, I stepped forward, but came to a sudden stop when my gaze found Pierce who stood with his head bent as he scrolled through his phone. He looked so panty-wettingly delicious with his black tousled mess of a hair pulled back and out of his face in its usual style. The light blue dress shirt he wore was rolled up at the sleeves, his suit jacket draped over one arm and a messenger bag hung on his shoulder. An angry scowl completing his sinful look.

I stood there like a deer as the doors began to close when he looked up and reflexively reached out to stop the doors from shutting me out.

"Are you coming in?"

"I... I... can wait for the next one," I stuttered lamely, because this elevator was so obviously filled to capacity. He pressed forward and snared an arm around my waist, pulling me in as the doors began to close again.

"What are you still doing in the office this late?" he asked, not letting me go, but instead held me against the wall by the panel of control buttons with the elevator bar pressing into my bottom. I really began to panic when he reached out a hand to hit the stop button.

"What are you doing?" I asked breathily, but didn't really care for an answer. I was surrounded by his heat and the hardness of his body made me dizzy with want. The steely wall of muscles, pressing me tightly against the wall. The sound of his messenger bag dropping to the floor along with his suit jacket in the quiet space brought my head back, but he was standing so close, and with my head barely clearing his shoulders, I was unable to meet his eyes.

He crouched down and roughly lifted my chin so that my lips were only a whisper from his. "Now I don't have to make up an excuse to see you tomorrow."

My chest heaved and pounded out of control. What were we doing? It was as if every encounter before this had merely been foreplay, leading up to this moment our bodies had already known to be inevitable.

"Have you missed me?" he asked.

I tried to shake my head, but with his hand firmly holding my chin in place, all I managed was an indecipherable croak.

He angled his head and slowly licked back and forth at my lips. "I haven't stopped thinking about you."

I moaned, feeling his hardness acquainting itself with my hip and stomach, and I wanted to open my mouth for him.

"Even while I was with another woman, all I could think of was your mouth on me."

"What?" The shock of his words registered in my voice. Why the fuck did he just share that with me? It was none of my business and I certainly didn't wish to hear any of it, but it definitely got my brain working again. Gripping at his sleeves, I attempted to pull him away from me and failed. He was like an immovable rock and with the four-inch heels I wore, my legs were shaky and unsteady.

"Ask me to kiss you," he barked at my lips, gripping tightly at my arms.

"Screw you! Get off me!" I said, so weakly. Every struggle of my body further exacerbated the heated feeling of the steel pipe between his legs, the length of it curving along my stomach and getting impossibly harder. Suddenly, he was yanking the hair at the back of my head and smashing his mouth to mine in a wet kiss that had me instantly surrendering. Veni, vidi, vici – he came, he saw, and he conquered.

I opened for him yet he roughly demanded more, our tongues dueling in a battle that left me in a defeated state of crying moans. I could hardly recognize myself.

"That's it baby," he crooned. "*Fuucck*. You taste like melting honey and victory."

He sucked and bit at my lips as his hands roamed my body. Pulling me forward, he slid his hands down the length of back to cup and squeeze my bottom in a grip so tight, I yelped in pain and moaned in pleasure.

"*Fuucck.* This ass. This ass that had me at hello."
He groaned.

I half giggled on a strangled moan. We were a hot mess of moans and groans.

His hands slowly made their way up the front of my shirt and roughly squeezed my breasts. "*Ahhhh.* I knew they were real. So firm. So soft. So fucking perfect," he said, trailing a path of soft kisses to my neck. Snipping and licking as he continued his assault on my breasts, squeezing harder and pinching my nipples.

I arched my back and clawed at him like a possessed animal. Good Gawd! I felt him everywhere. My skin burned as my body melted into him. His hands began unbuttoning my shirt as he feverishly kissed my neck. Parting my red shirt, his gaze narrowed on my breasts, my nipples painfully poking against the black lace cups of my bra. He impatiently yanked both cups down to latch his mouth to one pointed nipple. He repeatedly moved from one nipple to the other as if undecided on which he wanted most, all the while massaging and squeezing the swollen flesh.

"Aah," I gripped and pulled at his hair. "*Pierce*......aah."

"Uh...uh...agh... *Aiden*," I mumbled incoherently, willing myself to shut it.

"*Fuucck*. I want to come all over them," he said.

"You *are* a pervert," I moaned, my hands pulling his head further into my chest.

"Damn straight," he replied, biting down hard on my breast.

"Ahh!" I screamed. That was definitely going to leave a mark.

He pressed his forehead against mine as if trying to control himself. "Grip the bar."

"What?" I asked.

"*Grip* the fucking bar." He barked before taking my wrists and placing them on either side of me to grab onto the elevator bar behind me. "I need a taste. Hold on."

Chapter 11: Aiden

Fuck! I was losing my mind, but I had to get a taste of the honeyed vanilla scent that was damn near suffocating me. I hadn't meant to attack her in the elevator of all places, but I saw her and just like that, I had lost all logical thinking. She had been standing there like an offering on a silver platter in that red shirt that teased of the iniquitous delights beneath, her inviting mouth parting in surprise at my presence. My control vanished, taking all common sense along with it. She was both Eve and the damn apple and I was Adam going down for the count, not a single hope for redemption.

I dropped to one knee and pulled up the fitted skirt that accentuated the perfection of her ass, revealing a flimsy triangle of black lace that I could easily snap with one finger. Ripping the scrap of material, I lifted her foot to rest on my bent knee, completely baring her dripping pussy. I dove my head between her trembling thighs to lap up every heavenly drop, her scent leading me to the source of where my feast awaited.

Her fingers dug at my scalp. "Mmmm... *Aiden*... uhhh... *Pierce*... uhhh."

I chuckled at her cries, causing her to spasm as she gyrated her pussy deep into my face. "Aah...aah...aah... uhh..." Her sounds were a sweet cacophony of incoherency.

"*Aiden*.... I'm gonna come...... I'm gonna come." she threatened. "It's been too long.... too long.... *ohhh*.... that's soo good."

Too long since she had an orgasm? Or too long since she had been eaten? I didn't want to know. I plunged two fingers into her, dragging my tongue back and forth against her center. Gently biting, licking, and sucking. Moments later and all too quickly, her loud scream filled the small space and gradually tapered off into a chorus of soft moans. I sucked on her until trembling legs gave away her balance and she fell against me, her thighs straddling me. I grabbed her ass with both hands and slowly ground her pussy on my thigh to finish off her orgasm. She wrapped her arms tightly around my neck as her sweet sounds faded.

The startling sound of the elevator's alarm, blaring in its intensity, had her bolting out of my hold and throwing me off balance. She began righting herself, skirt and shirt were back in place, shoes that must have fallen off at some point were pulled on, and her disorderly appearance now looked less so. I stood to press the stop button, which stopped the alarm and briefly jolted the elevator before resuming its descent to the garage level.

I moved in behind her when she turned away from me, once again trapping her with my body. "When was the last time a man went down on you?"

Spinning around in my arms, she stared up at me. "As opposed to a woman?" she asked, sarcastically.

I exhaled a low chuckle and took her lips with mine, forcing my tongue into her mouth when she resisted. "Your pussy tastes so good, wouldn't you agree?"

She shoved away from me, tucking her blouse back into her skirt. "You're lucky there're no cameras in the elevators," she snapped.

I smiled at her and bent to pick up my things from the floor. "It would have made no difference." Holding up her tattered underwear, I said, "I'll get rid of these. And you're welcome."

She was flustered, biting on her pouty lips and flushing, even after what we'd just done.

"Come home with me," I heard come out of my mouth.

She started backing away from me and further into the elevator as the doors opened. "I believe this is your stop."

Ignoring her comment I asked, "Why are you still here?"

"I was taking a break from my emails to grab a snack when you interrupted."

"I believe *you* interrupted my trip to the garage. I was already on the elevator if I remember correctly." As the doors began to close, I pushed the button for the 19th floor, taking the ride back up with her. "Come on, let's grab your things. You're leaving." She started to say something, but I cut in. "You're leaving now, and I'll walk you to your car like a perfect gentleman." I raised a hand when she started again. "Please don't argue with me." She crossed her arms, drawing my attention to her chest. She glared and I smiled as we rode the rest of the way up in silence.

I followed Christen to her office where she collected her things and without further delay we were back on the elevator. "Where are you parked?"

"I take the subway." she said, pushing the button for the lobby. Judging from her body language, she was upset. More so at herself than at me.

"It's late. I'll drive you home," I said, and pressed the button for the garage. "Where do you live?"

"Tribeca," she said.

Luckily for me, she didn't argue. I was wound up and in several states of dissatisfaction. Our earlier prelude only served to inflame my hunger, and a specific body part of mine was not thrilled about it.

Once we exited the elevator, I pulled her to me by the waist and walked the short distance to my car. I opened the passenger door for her before taking the driver's seat, and soon after, we were exiting the garage and merging into traffic.

"You didn't answer my question," I said.

She rattled off directions to her place as I was about to miss the turn on West 83rd Street, before responding. "What question would that be?"

"When was the last time a man went down on you?"

"That's none of your business," she replied.

Rephrasing my question, I asked, "Is a man or *woman* currently warming your bed?"

"*Warming* my bed?" She laughed. "Isn't that a question you should've asked *before* you assaulted me in the elevator?"

"Judging from how tightly wound-up you were and how quickly you came, I'll take that as a no." I spared her a glance, but couldn't make out her expression through the darkened interior of the car, made even more so by the tinted windows.

She said nothing.

"What happened in the elevator will happen again, and again, and in more ways that get me hard just thinking about it. And you will love every second of the *assault*, as you so kindly put it."

I could have sworn I heard her utter, "*Oh My God*" under her breath.

"You can pull over around the corner there," she spoke, gesturing to a brick building while unbuckling her seat belt.

I pulled up to the curb and shifted gears into park. "If I didn't know any better I would think you were in a hurry to get away from me." Her smiling eyes told me I was right. "Don't I at least get a see-you-tomorrow kiss? Or you could just invite me in."

She opened the car door and slammed it behind her, soundly dismissing me.

Chapter 12: Chris

I WOKE UP THE NEXT MORNING feeling all kinds of aches. My breasts were sore and had marks all over, my neck sported matching bite marks, there were beard burns along my thighs, my legs still trembled, and my pussy throbbed for other reasons I didn't want to think about. The arrogant bastard had the gall to say it was going to happen again. *As if!*

Ok, yes. Of course, I wanted it to happen again. My mama didn't raise no fool! It had taken all of my willpower not to straddle him, pull out his hard cock, and ride myself into oblivion in the dark interior of his Range Rover last night. And if the earth-shattering orgasm in the elevator was a preview of what I could expect, then I would gladly beg him to take me any way he wanted.

However, these were thoughts I was definitely not going to let him in on.

I had only ever been in one serious relationship and that had been with Zander Morrison, my college boyfriend. I had slept with a few guys since then, but at 28 it was embarrassing to say I hadn't had an orgasm as explosive as I had with Pierce yesterday. Every single bit of his attention was focused on my pleasure. He possessed my body like he had a right to it, and I was more than eager to give him sole custody. And we didn't even have sex! Well, the penetration kind anyway.

I scurried to the bathroom, took a shower with a happy ending, and dressed for work in a yellow, navy and white striped pencil skirt and a navy short sleeve turtleneck to conceal the marks on my neck. I wasn't in the mood to take the subway, so I grabbed my phone to request an Uber and noticed a missed call from my brother Daniel. When my driver arrived, I hopped in and dialed him back.

"Hey, you!" I greeted when he answered.

"Hey, sis. Where are you?"

The driver easily maneuvered his way through the 7 a.m. Manhattan traffic as I spoke while trying to adjust my very tight ponytail. "On my way to work. What's up?"

"I'm in the city today. Can you do lunch?" Daniel asked.

"Sure, but it would have to be an early on. I have a 1:30 meeting."

"How about 11:30 or noon?"

"Yeah, either works." I replied. I normally took late lunches, except on the occasions I skipped breakfast or had back-to-back meetings. "Anything *specific* you want to meet about?" I inquired, knowing my brothers rarely came to the city on a weekday unless they had business meetings involving their BoxFlex gym in SoHo which wasn't too far from where I lived and where I enjoyed a lifetime membership. Or if there was a family emergency.

"Can't I just want to grab a bite with my baby sis?"

"No," I said.

He laughed "Nothing serious, just work stuff."

I suspected I knew exactly what "work stuff" he was referring to.

"Alright. We can meet at my office. Wanna grab a couple burgers from Melon's and bring over?"

"You got it." He said.

At the thought of Melon's amazing burgers, I was suddenly looking forward to a meeting where I knew my brother was going to make another attempt at getting me to come back to BoxFlex. "See you then."

"Later!" he replied, ending the call.

When I first started working with my brothers seven years ago, the gym had not been well-known or listed in any directory, which was unfortunate because the gym offered great services, most of which were free to youths who had parental consent. Their programs trained kids on basic self-defense techniques and skills for warding off bullies.

The gym had a lot of potential and I sought to change its lack of marketing by getting a website developed, creating social networking sites, and designing posters to display around campuses and even managed to get David and Daniel a spot on a local radio station to promote the gym which was a big help in getting them much needed publicity.

During the four-year period, I'd worked at the gym, my brothers and I forged a very close bond. The working experience and ideas we exchanged made my brothers see me not only as their baby sister, but also as a savvy career woman, and they credited me for putting the business on the map. I enjoyed working with them, but after completing my Masters I wanted to branch out on my own and work in a different industry. They supported me, but never gave up on pulling me back into their business.

I arrived at work, thanked my driver, and rushed into the building. My first order of business was to find Klaire, who was still not speaking to me. She had ignored the beautiful poem I sent and only responded to one of the 30 texts I'd sent since then with a, 'still not ready.' Well my patience had run out and so had her time!

Chapter 13: Aiden

"What the fuck is going on with you?" Lucas asked with a concerned expression.

We were having lunch at a restaurant not far from the office to talk shop and discuss the WingLing transition. I shook away the fog I had fallen into and took a bite of my steak.

"What do you mean?" I asked, clearing my throat. I'd barely heard a word of what he'd said for the past five minutes. My thoughts had temporarily been filled with a flimsy panty wearing woman.

"Have you heard anything I've said?" Lucas asked, taking a pull from his beer.

"Yes. You said we're getting rid of some dead weight in production and a few other guys in development who add no value."

He nodded in agreement. "I said that 30 minutes ago, but please continue."

"You're having Klaire Michaels draft a message to employees on PGE's corporate culture and you mentioned something about my disposition being shit."

He chuckled. "That was 15 minutes ago, what else?"

"Something about a press release on restructuring and rebranding?" That was when he had completely lost me as my mind wondered to the person who would be drafting it. I took a few more bites of steak so I didn't have to answer any more questions.

Lucas leaned back in his seat with an amused grin. "I had also said the waitress was flirting with you."

"I thought she was flirting with you."

"She brought two bottles of ketchup and gave both to you. I got fries too." He said.

"She shoved her tits in your face the entire time she was serving your plate," I countered, wiping my hands on my napkins as the waitress returned to the table.

"Can I get you boys anything else?" the waitress asked with a flirtatious smile.

"The check, please." I said.

"No, thanks." Lucas said at same time.

The waitress nodded, muttering she would be right back and then skipped away.

"Are we going to talk about what's got you so distracted?" Lucas asked.

"No," I said firmly.

"Ok. I know it's not about your father because he doesn't take up that much of your thoughts. And it's not about work, otherwise we would be discussing it, so that leaves one other guess," he said in mock contemplation.

I ignored him and pulled out my phone.

"Just tell me this woman is not who I think it is."

The waitress dropped off the check, and I reached for it so I didn't have to respond to Lucas, when a piece of paper with a phone number written on it slipped out. I returned the paper back to the check holder and paid in cash.

"Ready?" I asked, standing.

We grabbed our suit jackets and exited the restaurant.

Lucas did not drop the subject as we made the short walk back to the office. "We don't have a policy against interoffice relations, however, it's *still* ill-advised to date Chris." Lucas said. "And before you think about denying it, keep in mind I've seen the way you look at her and have noticed how you make her rewrite statements that are perfectly on point with our messaging." He stared at me sideways, daring me to deny it.

"*Christen* and I are not dating," I defended.

"Maybe not *yet*, but that's exactly where it's heading," he retorted. "And while we're on the subject, what are your thoughts on the position statement she drafted pertaining to the WingLing rebranding?"

Christen's informative rhetoric always had the ability to accurately capture the atmospheric temperature of any given event or issue, while also quelling lingering discourse with its decisiveness. "Very good. It communicates our objectives perfectly without alienating WingLing loyalists."

His smile was sinister and I wanted to punch it right off his face. "Excellent. We'll have it released by tomorrow afternoon."

I nodded my concurrence.

91

We reached our office building and stepped into the lobby. I paused briefly to take in the sight of Christen in a seemingly intimate embrace with a gentleman who looked to be very well acquainted with her as he placed a kiss to her forehead. Her back was to us so she hadn't seen us walking towards the elevators and stepping in. Lucas having also witnessed the display, raised his brow to me as if in question. I paid him no attention and impatiently pressed the button for the 20th floor.

"Let's hold off on the rebranding statement? I might have some changes in mind." I said once the doors opened and walked off to my office, not waiting for a response. I could make out Lucas's muttered obscenities, as well as a, "Here we fucking go again."

Back in my office, I was busy with few conference calls during which I couldn't help but wonder why Christen had allowed me to do such intimate things to her body yesterday when she was so clearly involved with someone. Not that I gave her much of a choice in the elevator, but she had plenty of opportunities to mention a boyfriend or lover, one of those times being when I specifically asked her if she was seeing someone, a question she never answered both times I asked. I had demanded a fucking answer, and would get one even if I had to force it out of her.

Two excruciating hours later, I sent Christen an email, politely demanding she come to my office at her earliest convenience. Shortly after, I was standing with both hands in the pockets of my black suit pants, staring out the floor-to-ceiling windows, enjoying the view and lost in thought when I heard a subtle knock on my door.

"Enjoying the view?" Christen asked, letting herself in. Her tone was playful.

Too bad I wasn't in the mood to play. "I need you to make changes to the rebranding position statement," I said abruptly, not turning to face her. The sound of her voice had the memories of yesterday flooding my mind and making me angrier than I already was.

"Ok. With which parts are you unhappy? Any specific lines you want reworded or taken out?" she asked, all traces of playfulness gone.

Good.

Why didn't she just tell me she had a boyfriend and worse, why had she let me kiss her, touch her? My gaze never strayed from the window, afraid that her information-withholding face would send me over the edge. I willed myself to remain calm, not sure how much longer I could continuing talking to glass.

"The parts on technology are a bit redundant and the paragraph referencing 'transformation' needs rephrasing," I said, grasping at straws.

When she said nothing, I glanced back then turned to face her. She was sitting in the same chair she had occupied the last time she was in my office, with her smooth legs crossed at the knees and her head tilted down as she scrolled through her phone with one high-heeled foot gently rocking back and forth.

Well wasn't she a cool customer? I hadn't ruffled a single feather. That was going to change. Her soft brown hair fell over one shoulder in waves, partially concealing her face, and I wanted to pull at it for denying me an unobstructed view. Her form fitting skirt rode up her thighs a little, making me want to explore what laid beneath, but all too quickly she interrupted my thoughts and she began reading from her phone.

"…The rebranding's main objective is to rebuild and restructure all WingLing series so that they align and conform to the high standards that have been set by PGE. Standards that have made PGE a visionary and innovative leader in the gaming technology industry…"

"Is this the part you have a problem with?" she asked, lifting her head before continuing to read another excerpt from the position statement.

"…and in the spirit of transparency, updates will be available on the company's website throughout the process as we continue to provide the superior value that sets us apart from our competitors…"

She lifted her eyes to mine with a puzzled expression. "Or is it this paragraph?"

"Change it!" I grated, illogically.

"I mean, isn't the end goal to capitalize on PGE's reputation?" she asked.

"Change it," I sneered. "I doubt it would take any effort for you and I'm sure you could come up with something equally as brilliant in your sleep," I muttered under my breath and without thinking.

Fuck!

She leaned back with a curious expression. "Was that a Freudian slip?"

My gaze fell to the swell of her breasts clad in black top that covered her neck, no doubt to hide the marks I left there. My jaw clenched in renewed anger and my pocketed hands balled up into fists as I slowly stalked towards her. Her eyes bore into me when I stopped mere inches from her chair.

"Why didn't you tell me you were seeing someone yesterday when I asked?" I barked. Her dating or fucking someone else changed absolutely nothing. I had been surprised at seeing her in the lobby with her lover, but that in no way changed my plans for her or the ways I planned to have her. She would just have to end things with him. Starting now.

Her eyes widened in confusion. "What?" She shook her head, still confused. "I'm not seeing anyone," she snapped.

I moved to lean in closer to her, hands braced on either side of the chair, caging her in. My voice dropping to a dangerously low whisper. "Then who was the man you had your arms wrapped around in the lobby?" I lifted her chin up with my thumb and forefinger so that her bewildered eyes met mine. "Are you fucking him?"

She uncrossed her legs and leaned forward so that our noses were nearly touching. "Is that what *this* is all about?" She asked, gesturing with one hand, her fingers tightly clutching her phone in the other. "That *man* is my brother, you insane asshole!" She said, gritting her teeth.

"We had lunch earlier and I must have been escorting him out when you saw us."

I stared back at her, completely stupefied.

"Cat got your tongue?" she taunted mockingly.

I slide my hand to the base of her skull to hold her in place for my attack as I crashed my lips to hers in a brutal kiss that left us struggling for breath. "I want you right now," I whispered into her mouth.

She chuckled, her breathing shakily. "That's too bad. I have a 4:30 meeting."

A quick look at my watch showed a time of 4:10. "Can't you reschedule it?" Not wanting to let her go, I kissed her again before she could respond, my hand sliding down her neck and gripping the base of her throat as her hands moved up my chest to grab onto my shirt. Squeezing her throat forcefully, I bit and sucked at her lips, my mouth stifling her moans. I forced myself to pull away, controlling my need to take her on the carpet.

"I can't reschedule it." she said, still breathing heavily. "I'm doing a news piece with Gaming Graphics Monthly and it was hard enough finding a suitable time that worked for all parties."

"I'm driving up to Pittsburgh in a couple of hours, but I'll be back Sunday afternoon." I said, loosening my tie and adjusting my shirt.

"Twelve hours on the road for a two-day trip?" she asked, fixing her hair and straightening her clothing.

"I need my car to move some things and depending on traffic, each way could be less than six hours."

"Ok, umm…. I gotta go, don't want to be late for my meeting. I'll see you Monday then?"

"I want to see you *Sunday* when I get back. I will text you," I said, moving over to my desk.

She walked towards the door before turning back. "So, you're fine with the position statement then?"

I smiled, not feeling or looking the least bit remorseful. "It will do."

She rolled eyes and said, "I don't know if I'll be available on Sunday."

"You'll make yourself available." I said firmly and added, "You forgot to thank me for the ride last night. I'll be collecting that on Sunday... *among other things*."

Spinning on her heels, she huffed and walked out. Was it bad business to get involved with her? Absofuckinglutely. Did I care? Not one bit.

Chapter 14: Chris

After a restless night of tossing and turning as thoughts of Pierce ran on an endless loop in my mind, I barely had enough energy for the workday ahead. Thinking of what happened in his office yesterday infuriated me, but still left me excited about Sunday even though I hadn't decided if I was going to see him. How dare he get jealous over my hugging another man when he admitted to being with another woman right before he assaulted my mind and body in the elevator? A subject I was yet to revisit with him.

Was *he* seeing someone? Did he plan on seeing them while he did whatever it was we were doing? Do I set some ground rules asking he not see anyone else? The way he made me feel was irrational. I didn't know much about him, yet my desire for him was so intense, leaving

102

my body to feel like it was meant to be joined with his. My attraction to men was normally based on intellect, some physical attributes and their treatment of me.

From working with Pierce so far, I could say that he was very intelligent and not to mention his work ethic and accomplishments spoke for themselves. He was so blatantly attractive in his demeanor and style, and his body was built in a way that I was used to with other men, but somehow with him I wanted to stop, stare, and slide my tongue all over him. His treatment of me, however, left a lot to be desired. Yet, somehow I didn't care that he wasn't very nice and often criticized my work. Of course, I wanted to see him, who was I kidding? As I readied myself for work, I decided I was definitely seeing him on Sunday.

Almost everyone looked forward to Fridays. For me it was just reminder of all the work I hadn't done during the week and how I'd have to stay late catching up. After spending more time on calls and in meetings than getting work done, it was a wonder anything gets accomplished. I got in at 6 a.m. and spent the whole morning and most of the afternoon, returning calls, responding to emails, organizing my calendar, and clearing up my inbox. I also managed to complete the rebranding content to be published on our website and social networking sites and sent out the press release. During all this, I barely thought of Pierce or what happened in his office yesterday, or the fact that I couldn't wait for Sunday, and I was proud of myself. At 3:30, I gathered up my materials for the comms bi-weekly meeting and headed to the conference room.

The meeting included the entire communications department along with Pierce and Hunt, both of whom joined via phone. We went around the room, with each person giving an update on what they had worked on during the week, as well as ongoing projects, upcoming events and news pieces, the good news, the bad news, road blocks, and any miscellaneous items. When Pierce began to ask questions and make suggestions in his deep gravelly voice, I had a flashback to his office yesterday, his knee-weakening kisses, his hold at my throat that had me creaming my pants. I couldn't wait to see him.

The meeting concluded with a Q&A session before everyone started to file out of the room. Still seated, I called out to Klaire, who had joined the meeting late. I had given her two-and-a half days of space, and her time had run out. She had to speak to me.

"Hey! Can you hang back for a bit?"

She paused on her way to the door, then walked over to join me. I smiled. She looked beautiful in a gray sheath dress. She was as partial to sheath dresses as I was to pencil skirts.

"I got your poem. It was ridiculous." She said, trying to bite back a smile.

"Hey, I put a lot of time into writing it," I joked.

"I'm sure you did," she said, rolling her eyes.

I would take her criticism over silence any day. "Are you still not speaking to me? Because I'm ready to hold you hostage in this room until you do. Or bribe you, anything you want. I'll even let you grab a boob or two," I teased, shaking my chest and winking, which probably looked like I was having a seizure. "Come on, you know you want to."

That got a laugh out of her, right before we heard the sound of someone clearing their throat. We both fastened our gazes to the conference speaker phone and froze. The green light indicating it was still on.

"Hello?" I asked, tentatively.

Hunt's voice came through the speaker. "Would you girls like some privacy?"

Our months opened in shock as Klaire and I looked at each other, not uttering a word.

"We thought we were alone!" Klaire eventually said, her irritation clear. "And why are *you* still on the line? The meeting ended five minutes ago."

A deep familiar chuckle filtered through the line, one that most definitely wasn't Hunt's.

Oh great, they were both still on the line. "*Pierce!*" I accused.

"If you wanted some privacy, perhaps you should have turned off the phone line," Pierce said, and Hunt chuckled.

"We didn't know it was still on. Perhaps *you* should have ended the call on your end. I'm assuming you two are together?" I asked, hoping Klaire and Lucas didn't think I sounded unprofessional then again, Klaire's question to Lucas hadn't been so professional either.

"Aiden isn't exactly my type, but we did take the call from the Pittsburgh office, if that's what you meant," Lucas confirmed.

Funny. I guess that dispelled the prima facie feelings I had regarding Lucas. I didn't know he had a sense of humor. "Clever. Thanks for letting us know. We're hanging up now."

"Before you do," Pierce added, "in the future you both might want to consider having your *grabbing* sessions outside of the meeting room."

Klaire and I gasped in unison as a chuckle I assumed belonged to Hunt flowed through the line. Pierce had a lot of nerve telling us to have our grabbing sessions elsewhere after what he did to me in the elevator. *Hypocrite!* I stretched over the table and hit the end button. Then we both burst out laughing.

"I think I really needed a good laugh." Klaire said, touching her stomach.

"Does this mean you forgive me and are speaking to me again?" I asked.

"There was nothing to forgive. I overacted and you were right to follow the confidentiality rules. I'm sorry I didn't respond to your texts, I've been a little stressed." She said, sounding somewhat defeated.

I shifted closer to her and took her hand. "Babe, what's going on?"

She shook her head. "It's…it's not a big deal. I need to go draft a memo. Let's talk later."

I nodded and released her hand. "Ok, wanna grab a drink after work?" I asked.

"Or ten," she said.

I laughed. "Sounds good to me."

CHAPTER 15: CHRIS

WE SIPPED ON OUR FIRST ROUND OF drinks as we hurried through the nearly crowded lounge to a high-top table that had just been vacated. The sophisticated lounge located on the terrace of a trendy hotel was lit like a Christmas tree with its mirrored lamp stands in various colors and glass stained lighting.

I took a few more sips of my pomegranate margarita and jumped right to it. "So, what's got you so stressed?" I crossed my legs and stared intently at Klaire.

"What's going on with you and Pierce?" she asked with a devious twinkle in her eye.

Her question took me by surprise for all of three seconds before I casually asked, "What do you mean?"

"What do you mean, 'what do I mean?'" she retorted.

"What do you think I mean?" I countered back.

She folded her arms and glared. "Seriously? Do you want to go another round?"

"Don't try and change the subject. I asked you a question first" I glared right back.

"You first!" She whined like a petulant child.

"Fine. You *infant*!" I conceded. "We kissed a few times."

"Aha!" she exclaimed, jerking forward as if she'd just caught me stealing candy from a baby. "I knew something naughty transpired between you two."

"Oh, please you knew nothing."

"Umm, based on your little gym run-in and the managers meeting foreplay, I'd say that was bound to happen. Now, I want every last juicy detail and no editing."

Oh fudge! I forgot I'd told her about my meeting with Pierce and Hunt. Sighing, I told her most of the details from the elevator incident, the car ride that followed and the rebranding meeting in his office yesterday. Klaire's eyes repeatedly went back and forth between wide and wider as I relayed everything. The version I shared was watered down from R to PG-13. A girl is entitled to a few naughty secrets.

She drained the rest of her Manhattan and fanned herself, even though the breeze in the terrace kept us pretty cool. "Wow, you've been a very bad girl, and I wholeheartedly approve."

"You would." I scoffed, rolling my eyes.

"It's about time you did a little less protestation and got a little more traction."

My laugh nearly choked me as I was downing my margarita. "You are completely cuckoo for cocoa puffs," I accused.

After a two-year hiatus, I'd have to agree with her. I had met guys I was attracted to, guys I wouldn't have minded sleeping with, but could never muster up the energy or commitment to do anything about it. After a while I got used to giving myself a helping hand and keeping my vibrator close at night. I liked that Pierce didn't give me the choice of protesting his advances or fighting my attraction to him, and the pull was only getting stronger each time I was around him. My body warmed under my composed exterior, and an animalistic need to have him possess me to the point of begging, took over my mind and body.

Klaire waved her hand to the waitress, signaling another round of drinks. "So, where does this leave you guys? Are you dating?"

"I think we're getting together on Sunday. I don't know the details yet, he's going to text me when he gets back from Pittsburgh. And I'm not looking to *date* him. He's my boss for crying out loud."

"Oh, you're just willing to fuck your boss. Yeah, that makes total sense," she said with sarcasm.

I sat up straighter in my stool with a feigned look of shock and gave her my best British impersonation. "Klaire darling, language. We're in public."

We both laughed, Klaire nearly falling off her stool as the waitress served another round of drinks. We chatted about work, the changes since the "merger-takeover" as we'd taken to calling it, how things weren't nearly as bad as the office had predicted, and Pierce's transparent and direct approach, as well as his no-bullshit management style.

"The office actually likes Pierce in spite of his permanent scowl, and employee morale has significantly improved. Who would have thought?" Klaire said, and I agreed.

"What number drink are we on?" I asked, feeling slightly tipsy and hungry.

"Four. You agreed to ten, so drink up," she replied, pointing a finger at me.

I picked up the menu to order food. "Will water and lemonade count? Because there's no way we're doing ten. What are we, frat boys?"

When the waitress returned, we ordered tuna carpaccio with avocado, mini crab cakes, a Tuscan kale salad with walnuts, and a wild mushroom pizza, all to share. We sipped our cocktails and took in the bustling crowd, and the cool spring breeze floated through the air as the music switched to a melodic trance song. When our meal was served, we dug in with gusto.

"Are we going to talk about what's stressing you out or just keep ordering drinks?" I gestured to Klaire with a slice of pizza before taking a big bite.

"I think Markus is fucking around," she said without pause, "which really sucks because we live together." Causally, she forked up some kale salad and chewed, like we were discussing the weather.

"Umm, not sure where to start with that. Do you mean sleeping with someone else or flirting? And what difference does living status make?"

She cocked her head to the side in thought before answering. "I'm not certain if he's sleeping with someone else, but I know something isn't right. I just have a feeling," she said, taking more bites of her salad.

"He's been distant and when I call, he doesn't answer. Instead, he calls back four to five minutes later. *Every time*. The other day he came home with this odd smell about him and waved it off when I asked what it was."

"Like another woman's perfume?" I asked. I've met Markus a handful of times over the one and a half years they've been dating. From what I could tell, Markus is a pretty decent guy and could be very vocal about his feelings when necessary. He didn't strike me as someone who would cheat or sneak around.

"That's what I thought, but he said I was being ridiculous." She paused to sip her drink. "It sucks because the apartment is his, which means I would have to find a place if this goes south."

"You know you can always come live with me and I'm sure that wouldn't be the *only* reason you'd be upset if he were cheating. Right?"

She sighed. "I think we've both been unhappy for some time, and the stale sex isn't holding the Band-Aid in place anymore. We're just too chicken to hurt the other person's feelings by admitting it."

"Hmm," I said. "I say just rip the Band-Aid off all together."

"But I don't want to be homeless. It's a nightmare trying to find a decent place in the city."

I laughed. "You're ridiculous! I just offered you my place, so stop being a drama queen." I leaned away from the table as our server returned to refill our water glasses. "How is your dad holding up? Are the treatments taking?" I asked when the server left.

Klaire's dad was diagnosed with lung cancer almost three years ago, and as a lifelong smoker, his prognosis hadn't been good. To say Klaire and her dad have a rocky relationship would be putting it mildly. Her dad had walked out of her life when she was nine years old, after her mother had passed, leaving her to be raised by her grandparents. With less than a year to live, he reconnected with Klaire to ask her forgiveness and make amends. And despite her claims of wanting nothing to do with him, I knew it affected her.

"He's doing as well as someone who's going to be dead any day now. My faux step-mother or whatever the fuck she is, and her son, have been at his bedside, playing the parts of the concerned family members." Shrugging, she took gulp of water. I suspected it was because her margarita glass sat empty. "I'm sure he's in good hands," she finished bitterly.

Her dad and his girlfriend were to get married months prior to his diagnosis, but were forced to postpone the wedding as a result of the cancer treatments, and have remained unwed.

"I'm sorry babe," I said, taking her hand and squeezing before letting go.

"It's fine. You know we were never close and he's still a son of bitch. Dying isn't going to change that." The inflection in her voice belied her coldly spoken words.

We ordered another round of drinks as the dishes were cleared, vowing it would be the last. "I'm still hungry," I blurted out and we both laughed. "Why the hell did we order chick food?"

Klaire held up an accusing hand, still laughing. "You did most of the ordering."

We debated for a few minutes, eventually placing another order of kale salad, lamb chops and fries. Moment later, a couple guys in suits came up to our table to flirt. They sported cheesy grins and even cheesier pickup lines, both of which we dismissed on account that we were "waiting on our psycho boyfriends to join us."

Returning to our earlier conversation, I said, "I think you should gather up some balls and end things with Markus if you're both unhappy, rather than dragging this out any further. You're not exactly a wallflower when it comes to having your way, and Markus knows this."

"I know you're right, I'm just not ready and if he is cheating, I'd like to be certain of it."

"If things are not working, would it make a difference if he weren't cheating?"

She shook her head. "No, but I would want us to remain friends if I can help it."

"Ok. My offer stands. You know I'm here for you no matter what." I stood and gave her a brief hug. "I'm going to the restroom. Be right back."

When I returned, Klaire went next. I retrieved my phone and saw I had four text messages from Pierce and two from my brother David. I guess it was David's turn to request a lunch meeting. I tapped on Aiden's name and read his texts.

[8:17pm] Aiden: I hope you're not working late. You're going to need all the rest you can get before Sunday.

[8:22pm] Aiden: What do you say to dinner? At my place.

[8:31pm] Aiden: Make it easy on both of us and don't wear any panties when you come. To dinner that is.

I let out a bark of laughter and sent a reply.

[9:20pm] Me: I'm not sure how comfortable I'll feel about dinner at your place if it's sans lingerie.

Klaire reappeared as I was putting my phone away. "What are you grinning at?"

"Nothing."

"Uh huh, sure," she said, but didn't press for details.

During the hour that followed, we shamelessly enjoyed our second meal and chatted about BoxFlex, my unrelenting brothers, and their plans to open two new locations.

"Don't forget you're living in Daniel's condo, so you might want to be a little nicer to him. It's also lucky that you at least have that option as a fallback plan," Klaire commented, her expression solemn.

I dabbed my napkin to my lips, trying to process her words. "Fall back plan for what?"

"In case things don't work out at PGE," she said matter-of-factly.

Tensing, I dropped the napkin and took a sip of water. "Why wouldn't things work out at PGE?" I asked, knowing exactly where she was headed.

She shrugged. "You know, *if* things got weird between you and Pierce."

It was a subject I'd purposely not wanted to think about, much less voice out loud. "Thanks for putting it mildly and I do see your point, but hope that when the flirtation between Pierce and I wears off or ends, that we'd continue on like civilized adults."

Klaire's narrowed eyes spoke volumes. It said that had been the most impressive load of BS she'd ever heard, and that she admired how I managed to say it with a straight face.

I straightened my shoulders and continued down the path towards lala land. "We're just flirting, it's not a big deal, besides he travels a lot, and once the merger is finalized, we probably won't see so much of each other."

When she simply stared back me, not articulating a single thought, I got defensive and leaned in over the table. "Look here, missy!" I said, pointing a finger at her. "I recall you saying you 'wholeheartedly approve' of our shenanigans and thereby proving your complicity. *Do you deny this?*"

Her face fell as she spoke in a low whisper. "You're right, I did say that."

"Please speak into the mic so the jurors can hear you," I snapped.

"Now you look here, *you crazy person*, I don't know what you've been smoking, but you need to lay off the crack pipe!" She snapped back.

We stared at each other for a beat, then burst out laughing.

Composing myself, I wiped away tears of laughter that slid down my face. "Sorry. I started the SVU marathon. I guess I got carried away."

"You think?" she asked, still laughing. "I'm sorry. I shouldn't have said that about Pierce and PGE. I want you to let loose and get laid while you're at it, but I also don't want to see you hurt by him. In this scenario, you stand to lose a lot more than he does."

"Believe me, I know you're right," I said.

We were silent as our table was cleared, our moods sober and contemplative.

"There's no denying Pierce is a total slice, and I would probably risk it too," Klaire said, breaking the silence. "You should have a conversation about your 'flirtations' before the waters get murky."

"Total slice?" I grinned. "I think we went way past *murky* in the elevator."

"A slice of heaven," she said, wiggling her brow.

"Ah. Of course. Silly me, how did I not get that," I said sarcastically.

She stifled a laugh and rummaged through her purse. "What are you doing tomorrow?"

I sighed. "Gym, cleaning, laundry, some errands, airport lunch, and hopefully, I can fit in a wax-scaping."

She pulled out her phone and tapped rapidly at the screen. "Airport lunch?"

I shuddered, either from the cool breeze or at the thought of making a trip to Queens. "Jenna has a layover in New York and I promised to meet her for brunch."

Jenna Speckerman was my college roommate freshman year and also my sorority sister. We used to be close until one night, during our spring break trip to Cabo junior year, her "casual" drinking had taken a turn for the worst. She had gotten so drunk and ended up slipping into my brother's bed. Matthew, who was also vacationing with us, hadn't been very pleased and neither was Nicole, his girlfriend at the time. Her drinking had bordered on excessive and often led to events that would have serious consequences for me as well. Once, she received a one-week suspension from school after she snuck a bottle of wine into the library during a study session. All my efforts to curb her enthusiasm were in vain, and after that night in Cabo, justifying a relationship with her became difficult. When we returned to the city, I made it clear that she needed to talk to her parents and get some help. And after our talk, she had stopped speaking to me.

Since then, she had reached out, making numerous attempts to resuscitate our friendship and I'd given her a chance. We kept in touch, though we were not as close as we had once been. She appeared to have turned over a new leaf, and I liked the alcohol-free Jenna. She currently resided in Las Vegas, having moved there with her fiancé after graduation, but made frequent trips to New York and insisted on a meeting every time. I was happy to oblige.

"I was hoping we could get a massage, maybe a mani/pedi. I need some pampering," Klaire said, bringing me back to the present.

A massage sounded heavenly. Wanting to accommodate her, I suggested a possible solution. "How about I do my cleaning and laundry tonight, and then tomorrow after the gym we could get a massage, mani/pedi and wax-scaping for moi, before I meet with Jenna. You could also come along and finally meet her." With the clock approaching 10 p.m., I was in for a long night, which I'd be paying for in the morning.

Her face was overcome with excitement, making me smile. And just like that, the long night ahead was worth it. "What about your errands?"

I waved a dismissive hand. "Not important." I didn't need a new dress or lingerie to have dinner with Pierce. In fact, he requested I not wear any.

"Why is the wax-scaping only for you? Maybe I want one."

I scrunched my face at her pouting expression. "What's with the duckface? Are you trying to make me lose my dinner?"

Her head fell back in a fit of giggles. "Shut up!"

"You don't need waxing my pretty, because you're *not* getting laid," I said in a voice that sounded like the Wicked Witch of the West. I immediately ducked when a napkin came flying towards my head.

"You're so mean to me, but I love you anyway," she croaked, feigning sadness.

Chuckling, I threw the napkin back at her. "That's because you like a little pain with your pleasure. Don't you, little girl?"

"You're nuts," she sighed. "If you're gonna be cleaning and doing laundry tonight, we better get out of here. It's getting late."

I signaled for the waitress and stood to stretch. "It *is* late."

"What are your 'not important' errands anyway?"

"I was thinking lingerie shopping since it's been *awhile*, and maybe a little black dress."

"And that's not important because you'll be meeting Pierce naked on Sunday?"

"Something like that," I muttered under my breath.

We paid the bill and made a trip to the restroom before taking a cab to our respective homes.

Chapter 16: Chris

Saturday turned out to be a whirlwind of activities. I managed to get the cleaning and laundry done the night before, but not nearly enough sleep. Pierce and I texted into the morning, up until I passed out, which must have been some time before his last texts.

[2:03am] Aiden: How wet are you right now?

[2:05am] Aiden: I hope you sleep naked because I don't allow clothes in my bed.

[2:11am] Aiden: Did you pass out on me?

I sent a response at 8 a.m. when I'd awoken, stating I indeed had passed out. Our texting continued through my morning workout, my pampering session with Klaire, and brunch with Jenna. I was grateful Klaire had decided to come along for that. For their first meeting, they had gotten along a lot better than I could have expected. Jenna had regaled us with plans for her upcoming nuptials and invited us to the bachelorette party taking place in the Bahamas a few months from now. As wonderful as a weekend trip to the Bahamas sounded, I was a little hesitant making a commitment on the spot, and promised to think it over. Klaire and I were also able to squeeze in some shopping after lunch. I purchased some lingerie and three dresses because a girl could never have too many of those. Twelve hours later, I crashed for the rest of the day.

By Sunday morning, I was very much relaxed and well rested, not to mention the massage we had on Saturday did wonders to release the tension in my shoulders. The text exchanges between me and Pierce the past couple of days made me feel more comfortable with what we had planned for today. I felt like I was beginning to him know better, which made this 'dinner date' appear less sordid in my mind. There was a lot of flirting and sexual innuendo, but we also discussed how he started PGE 12 years ago, and his move back to New York, in as much detail as we could over text.

I was going to be missing Sunday dinner with my parents, so I placated them by making a trip to Brooklyn to deliver a basket of baked goods from my mom's favorite bakery in the city. My mom was her usual charming self as she began her routine of criticizing my singlehood with lectures of finding a "decent" man to settle down with, and how I won't find a man if I was constantly working, because "men find successful independent women intimidating." I wished my mother wouldn't take my being single as a personal affront or attack on her. I especially wished I had the nerve to tell her my plans of having intimate relations with a hot man all night and the reason I would not be making it to dinner, rather than the lie I told them of having to work. My dad, however, was far less critical. He was very supportive of my career and only wanted me to be happy. He practiced law for most of his life and made partner at a corporate law firm where he'd met my mother, a paralegal at time. He later left the firm to serve in the Justice Department before retiring four years ago. My brother Matthew followed in our father's footsteps by pursuing a career in law. My family was no stranger to hard work, and having three very successful older brothers motivated me. My career was my focus and if I happened to have good sex with Pierce along the way, then all the better, and I'd enjoy it while it lasted. I didn't desire or need anything more.

Around 3 p.m., I received a text from Pierce with his address and instructions he left with the concierge to program my prints for access to his elevator. I was giddy and nervous, and couldn't help but wonder if that meant I'd be making future trips to his place. We agreed on a 4 p.m. meeting time, but with the subway delay en route from my parents', it was safe to say I'd be running late.

Once I got home, I took a shower and pulled on one of the new dresses I'd purchased. It was a black strapless number made of a super-soft jersey material with a lace hem insert that fell to mid-thigh. It molded to my body perfectly, emphasizing my pert breasts and derriere. I styled my hair in its naturally wavy form, letting it fall loosely down my back. My makeup was lightly applied with a deep-brown eyeshadow and a soft matted lip cream. Finishing off my look, I pulled on a pair of black velvet heels with two thin straps, one glided over my toes and the other buckled at my ankles. I pulled on a knee-length purple trench coat and dashed out of my building to hail a cab.

It was 4:23 p.m. by the time I arrived at Pierce's luxurious apartment building. A man by the name of Mack escorted me to a desk where he programmed my fingerprints into a flat panel LED screen before leading me into the private elevator. I was a bundle of nerves as the elevator took me on a ride, stopping on the 78th floor. The doors opened into a marble foyer leading up to the apartment's entrance, and before I could lift a finger to the bell, the door swung wide open. My breath caught at the sight of Pierce standing there in a pair of drawstring sweatpants. His broad shoulders and solid chest were encased in a loose-fitting t-shirt that failed to disguise his defined physique. The clean smell of either cedarwood body wash or shampoo filled my nostrils when he suddenly grabbed my upper arm, pulling me into him before he shut the door and slammed me against it. Bending slightly at the knees, he slid one hand to the back of my head while the other gripped at my throat as his mouth came crashing down to mine. His tongue and lips ate at my mouth as he applied pressure to my throat. I tossed my purse to the floor and clutched at his damp hair in a white-knuckling grip, further fueling his ravishment.

"Hello. You're late," he said, licking the swells of my breasts.

I moaned out an apology.

His lips slid back to mine for a quick kiss before he pulled back to take off my coat. "Would you like a tour?" he offered, bending to pick up my purse and placing it on a small table beside the coat closet.

I nodded, catching a breath to orient myself to the surroundings. The high-ceilinged, open space was stunning and very…. *empty*. "Did you get robbed?" I teased.

He chuckled and took me by the hand. "I bought the place last week and plan to hire a decorator at some point. The master bedroom, game room, and kitchen are the only furnished rooms at the moment."

I followed as he led me into the living room that featured a fireplace, a fully-stocked bar area with glass sliding doors that opened into a beautiful terrace, floor-to-ceiling windows spanning throughout the apartment, showcasing spectacular views of the city, and an Lshaped staircase that led up to the second level. The marble flooring gleamed beneath a set of dim recess lighting, casting the space in a warm glow. As we walked through the spacious areas, Pierce offered commentary on the various artwork on displayed. The sleek kitchen was equipped with enough stainless-steel cookware and gadgetry to make a top chef contestant envious.

Dropping my hand, he moved to the open the fridge. "Would you like a drink?"

I spun around slowly on my heels, admiring the classically elegant space. "Lemonade or ginger ale if you have either."

He pulled out a glass bottle of ginger ale and poured some into a tumbler. "That's very specific."

Smiling, I rounded the kitchen island and climbed onto one of the high chairs. "Even your ginger ale is fancy," I commented, and took the drink he handed me.

He swiveled my chair to face him and pulled my legs apart to accommodate himself between them. "How so?"

"I didn't know ginger ale came in cute glass bottles," I said, taking a thirsty sip.

"My housekeeper stocked the kitchen. I can have her get you some if you'd like." His eyes were on my lips as his hands slid up my thighs, hiking my dress further up. "Are your desires always so specific?"

I placed the tumbler on the kitchen island and ran my hands up and down his ropey arms. "No, not always. Sometimes, I haven't a clue what I desire."

"Is that so? Perhaps we could experiment with a few options," he said, whispering into my ear as his fingers moved dangerously close to my center.

"I thought we were having dinner." I argued even as my body reacted to a hunger that was entirely different.

Hs brought his mouth to mine and pulled my thighs closer to his hardness. "After."

"After what?" I whispered, closing my eyes and feeling the brush of his lips, then the sweep of his tongue. This kiss was slow, painfully so, and incredibly sensuous.

"After I give you a tour of the bedroom," he said.

I squealed when he hoisted me up against his body and rounded the corner to take the stairs.

As he dropped me to my feet, I barely had the chance to take in the ginormous space when Pierce ordered me to sit. I walked over to the large bed and sat down with my hands splayed on either side of me, feeling the welcomed coolness of the duvet beneath my palms. He was standing several feet away from me, his beauty competing with a view that overlooked the Empire State Building.

"Move to the edge and pull up your dress. I want your legs wide open," he commanded.

A surge of lust had me immediately complying, and in that moment, I would have done anything he asked of me. I fell into a trance as he slowly pulled off his shirt before tossing it to the floor, revealing a body contorted with steely lean muscles and a stomach riddled with speed bumps. The light dusting of dark hairs trailing down and into his pants towards a massive protrusion that had my lower body seizing involuntarily.

"Open your legs wider. I don't want anything impeding my view," he barked gruffly.

My legs open wider of their own volition, and his piercing gaze on my pussy had it clenching desperately.

Gripping tightly on the duvet, I licked lips that were getting drier with every passing minute. My vision was hazy as I watched him reach into the waistband of his pants to fist the protrusion that was demanding freedom and attention.

"What would you like?" he teased with lust-filled eyes.

I swallowed hard and teased his right back. "What's on the menu?"

A devious smile played on his lips. "*Everything.*"

The all-consuming need that coursed through my nerve endings was blinding. I wanted *everything* he offered, in no particular order, and preferably all at once, if possible.

"In that case, I want to suck on your cock like it's my favorite blow pop," I hurriedly spat out the words like they were going out of style.

With his hand still fisted around his cock, Pierce strode towards me like a panther, like I were his prey, and anything short of total destruction would be unacceptable. He stopped with his crotch at my face and brought the hand that had been gripping his cock to my chin, lifting it with his forefinger and using his thumb to smear precum back and forth across my lips. My tongue instinctively darted out to lick my lips, swiping his thumb in the process.

"Good choice," he praised, "but how about I eat that pussy that's making a mess on my sheets first?"

Unable to speak, I nodded rapidly like a bobble head, thinking he may change his mind. His low chuckle sounded more like a groan, and without further ado, he crouched down and dove mouth first into my wetness. He licked up and down my folds as I fell to my back, my hands pulling at his hair without care as he snipped and sucked. The scruff of beard made the tonguing that much more intense, and when his finger plunged into me, I thought I would combust. The pressure was too much, yet so good.

"Aah……aah…. I'm coming." I fought the urge to ride his face, wanting this to last for hours.

He hiked my leg over his shoulders and fucked me harder with his mouth and fingers. "I missed your pussy," he groaned. "So intoxicating." His fingers dug into my ass and lifted me higher to lap up my juices like he were drinking from a bowl.

"I can't *Aiden*, it's too…." My breathing became harsher with each tongue thrust as I slowly began to ride his face. When he smeared my juices to my back entrance and slid a finger in, I was completely done for. My screams sounded hoarse, even to my ears as I bucked and spasmed out of control. The climax seemed to go on forever as he massaged the outer layers of my sex while still fingering my rear.

"Oh gawd oh gawd …. what did you do?" I moaned accusingly. The pleasure was so intense, I could have sworn there were fireworks prickling behind my eyelids.

Moments later, he was pulling at the top of my strapless dress and bared my breasts. I sat up to assist him, yanking it off before leaning over to remove my heels, but he was already there, flinging them to the side. When he stood, I reached for his sweatpants and pulled. His mushroomed cockhead poked out and stared angrily back at me. I licked my lips and swallowed. Pierce stepped out his pants once I had managed to pull them down his feet, then moved out of my reach.

"Later," he grumbled. 'I need inside you now."

He grinned when I pouted my lips in disappointment, and strode into an adjoining room that I could only assume was the bathroom. My eyes were glued to his beautiful form, his corded back narrowed down to twin dimples that highlighted the perfection of his ass. It was like poetry in motion. He returned a second later with an unopened box of condoms and impatiently ripped it open before moving over me on the bed. He anchored an arm around my upper back and pulled our joined bodies up towards the pillows. Propping his upper body on his elbows, he bracketed mine and softly kissed my lips as he nudged my legs further apart. Our tongues tangled, slow and wet, his mouth sure and aggressive. My head pressed harder into the pillow when I felt his mouth on my breasts, kissing and licking. I groaned when his teeth pulled on a nipple, sucking and biting painfully, and exacting the same treatment on the other. I arched my back to push my nipples further into his mouth as I slid my hands into his hair to massage his scalp, my moans getting louder with each pull of his teeth.

"Your tits are so fucking perfect, big and ripe," he groaned. "I thought of them all weekend, of sucking them, fucking them and coming all over them."

I'd never had a man pay so much attention to my breasts during sex, beyond the usual fondling and groping, maybe a brief suck here and there. I also never gave it much thought. Pierce's attention and ministrations left me wet, desperate and needy. I craved it now and was on the precipice of another climax. I groaned at the pain of his assault and moaned at the sweet pleasure.

"You want me to cum all over them," he said as a statement of fact.

The hands that were massaging his scalp had long stopped and were pulling at the strands. "Yes," I moaned.

"Later. I need inside your melting pussy now," he said, retrieving a condom and ripping the foil apart before rolling it on.

I laughed. "You keep saying that."

He leaned over me with one arm braced beside my head and the other gripping my thigh to rest against his in an upward angle. "Your body is a fucking distraction. So many thing I want to do first."

I brought his month to mine and gently bit his bottom lips.

"Put him inside. Now," he barked.

I dragged my nails down his arm and reached between our bodies to guide his thick length into me. My gaze locked with his midnight blues that were so piercing and so demanding as it made promises I knew he would deliver.

Chapter 17: Aiden

I SLOWLY BEGAN THRUSTING forward into her soaked cunt, but was having a hard time getting very far.

"*Fuck,*" I growled. She was tighter than a fist ready to throw a punch and my balls drew up in excitement. I pistoned forward, a little harder this time, and made some progress. "You're not a virgin, are you?"

The sound of her laugher was like a sweet melody to my ears. "No," She exclaimed, her laugher fading into a soft moan.

151

I thrusted more forcefully, my cock pulsing like it had a heartbeat of its own, my strokes short and deep until I plunged in all the way.

"Aah," her hands slid up my back to clamp around my neck as she lifted herself up to meet my thrusts. "I'm so full, fill me up Aiden, fill me up."

"You are going to take every fucking inch." I pounded harder into her.

"Yes," she groaned, her eyes falling shut.

"Look at me," I demanded. My strokes were brutal and unrelenting. I couldn't get enough of this heavenly feeling. Her pussy strangling my cock in a fierce grip as she tried to keep up with my hard thrusts, almost had me coming. It was too soon, I needed more of this, more of her, more of the exquisite pain that had my balls in a vice. I didn't want to come. I wanted to fuck inside her for hours, days. She felt like a dream. When she dug her nails into my ass, I jerked further into her, if that were even possible. I was in her so far and deep that my cock had enough leverage of its own to lift her right off the bed. I had to slow down, but I couldn't.

Her loud moans and quivering pussy alerted me to her fast-approaching climax. I leaned forward, my chest pressing into her as I fisted the sheets at either side of her head and fucked mercilessly into her. The root of my cock ground into her pubic bone, causing her folds to ripple around me. I felt a sharp and sudden pain piercing into the skin of my arm when a loud strangled cry filled the space between us. She climaxed around my cock, bucking and frantically shaking her head from side to side, like I was an exorcist purging out her demons all the while, she threatened to take me down with her. She whimpered softly as her pussy quivered around me, and eyes drunkenly shut. I slowed down the pace of my thrusting and watched her return to the land of the living. Gently, I pulled out midway before sliding back in, in a rhythm that had her sighing in pleasure. I didn't want to overstimulate her sensitive nerves, and I needed the opportunity to collect myself to avoid losing it completely. She was stunning, her hair a beautiful tangled mess, her eyes half closed with a smile tugging at swollen puffy lips and her perfect tits bouncing with each thrust as her pointed nipples begged for my mouth.

Fuck me! I was dying and loving every torturous second.

She dazedly slid a weak hand up my arm. "I'm sorry I bit you."

My gaze shifted to the hand where she touched a furious looking bite mark. "I know of a few ways you can make up for that." I said, leaning down to kiss her.

"So do I." She said, her smile widening.

I pulled back a little so I could see her face better while I continued to thrust slowly into her. "Yeah? Let's hear it?"

She cupped her breasts and began massaging. "I could suck on you until you were ready to come all over me."

Fuck me!

She was killing me softly and had me picking up the pace. "I was already going to do that. You can't offer me something I'm already collecting."

She whimpered, her voice shaking as she spoke. "True, but it would be an I-owe-you to be used in the future." Lifting up on both feet, her hips rose to meet mine while her fingers moved to pinch her nipples.

I was losing it. I couldn't hold out for much longer. And why the fuck were we having a conversation in the middle of fucking? I banged into her with each word I spoke. "You will suck me off. *Whenever* I want. And I will come on your tits, your ass, down your throat or anywhere else that pleases me." Gripping her wrists, I pinned them to the bed. I leaned forward and pounded. Hard. I was done talking.

Our mating was too good and I was going to explode, the pleasure overwhelmed my senses, driving me to a point of no return. My balls clenched, my spine tinkled, and my cock began to spill. Digging my knees into the mattress, I fucked her hard and deep.

Her cries were pleasantly deafening, strung together in a series of *"Fuck me...so fucking good Pierce.... yes Aiden.... Aiden.... don't stop..."* The beautiful symphony of my name on her lips, crying out in desperation as her pussy choked and pulsated on my cock was more than enough to send me to the bottom of the ocean, drowning out every coherent thought as I flooded her pussy with my come. And still I hammered on, not wanting to let go. I collapsed on top of her when the pulsing of her cunt slowly came to stop. Our bodies misted with sweat and our hearts beat steadily as I wondered how soon we could go again.

I couldn't recall ever being with someone and wanting to fuck for as long as possible. The goal usually being, get it, make it good for her, come, get out, go home. With Christen, I wanted to get in, make the good never stop, come, stay in and go again. I wanted to fuck her fifty ways to Sunday and afterwards, hit repeat.

I lifted myself from her limp body. Gripping the base of the condom, I slowly pulled out of her. "Fuck!" I barked, startling her.

She rose up on her elbows and looked at me with half lidded eyes. "What is it?"

Even in my panic, my gaze still managed to roam her naked body. "I broke the condom." I muttered, raising off the bed and heading straight to bathroom. This was obviously my fault. I'd had the feeling of pouring into her when I climaxed, but kept pumping away. I threw what was left of the condom into the toilet and flushed, and was reaching into the large frameless glass shower that offered no privacy by design, when Christen came in behind me.

"If you're worried about STDs, don't be. I had a full physical, two years ago, and I haven't been with anyone since. Well, besides you."

I was surprised and momentarily frozen. *Two years*? No wonder she'd felt like a fist and been virgin-tight. I reached into the shower and switched on the multi-head spray before turning to face her. She was still as naked as I was and just like that, I wanted her again.

"Get in." I said, taking her hand and bringing her under the shower spray. I came up behind her, lathering shower gel along her sinful body.

"I'm not on the pill." She blurted out after a few minutes.

My massaging hands stilled in her scalp. "What?"

"I know society would have you thinking every single woman has been on the pill right from birth," she said with sarcasm, "but I have regular periods and I wasn't having sex, so I didn't see the point of staying on a medication I didn't need."

"So, you're telling me you *could* get pregnant?" I asked, trying to remain calm, but furious at myself for being so reckless. As a teenager, I had been inside a girl without protection so of course I knew how great it felt, but I'd never come inside one, by accident or on purpose, and it was certainly not something I practiced into adulthood. My relationships, if you could call them that, were strictly sexual and never lasted beyond a couple of months. I had no reason to have unprotected sex and used condoms religiously. I didn't know how I would feel about a pregnancy. I only hoped she wasn't pregnant, because I wasn't up to dealing with that any time soon.

"I'm fairly certain I'm not given the time of month. I should be getting my period in the next 4-5 days."

Turning her to face me, I lifted her chin. "I don't know if I like those odds. I want you on some form of birth control as soon as possible."

She remained silent, squeezing gel in her hands and slowly running it along my chest and arms before speaking. "What are we doing here? I don't want this to interfere with work."

I leaned in to kiss her, my hands sliding my hands down to massage her beautiful breasts. I've always been an ass man, never cared too much for tits, but hers were too fucking perfect to be ignored. I was becoming obsessed. And she did have a great ass, one that elicited all kinds of debaucheries.

"We're taking a shower. And it won't." I said, moving to kiss down her dripping wet body until her pussy was in my face. I wanted to distract us both. She pulled away when my tongue licked at her clit.

"It's my turn," she said, falling to her knees and reaching for my cock.

Leaning over the shower panel, I activated the steam function and pulled her up to take a seat on the low built-in bench. I stroked my cock and lifted the head to her lips. "Here you go. I don't think I could deny you anything."

She moaned and eagerly covered the head with her mouth, stroking up and down the length. "Tell me how you like it," she said, looking up at me and breaking my heart with the fierce need I felt for her.

I swept her wet hair away from her face and gripped it at the back. "Your wicked mouth is already killing me."

She darted her tongue out and licked her way down, sucking along every straining vein.

"Just like that," I groaned when her tongue swirled around the head and dipped into the small slit. Her sweet suckling tightened my balls as she attempted to take the entire length down her throat.

"*Fuck.*" The vibrations from her moans had me moving forward and pumping furiously into her mouth. "Relax your throat, baby," I encouraged, and let out a harsh groan when she complied. "That's it baby. You can take more, I've got a lot more to give you."

Her moans got louder as she took me in, all the way to the hilt. Pulling back after long minutes, she swallowed and took my balls into her mouth and sucked hard as I pumped my cock. It felt so good, but my greedy cock wanted back in. I pulled at her hair to release the death grip her mouth had on my balls and pushed my cock back in. The guttural sound I emitted was foreign to me.

"Open up baby and suck hard," I choked out.

She took me all the way down, relaxing her jaw as I began to pump down her throat and groaned when her nails dug into my glutes.

"Christen baby, I'm coming," I warned, barking out a string of curses. "Drink me up," I groaned and began releasing down her throat. Pulling out, I pumped the last stream of come on her tits and watched her massage it into her plump flesh.

"*Fuck*. And you say I'm perverted."

She looked up at me through the fog of steam, a sly grin playing on her lips. "You're rubbing off on me. *Pun* very much intended."

I chuckled and leaned down to kiss her swollen lips. "You filthy girl. You love having my come all over you, don't you?"

"Yes," she smirked. "And now you need to feed me the dinner you promised."

CHAPTER 18: AIDEN

WE TOWELED OFF AND GOT DRESSED in the bedroom. I threw on the sweats and tee from earlier while Christen walked into my closet to pull on one of my dress shirts. I'd never brought a woman back to my place since I started living on my own, in Pittsburgh or anywhere else for that matter. I always opted to go to their place for various reasons and on occasion suggested a hotel. My home was my private sanctuary, and having Christen in my personal space was intimate, too intimate, and I wasn't sure how I felt about that. The thought hadn't even occurred to me as too personal when I asked her to dinner, and I was sure I wouldn't hesitate to invite her back.

"Your closet is huge. I'm guessing bigger than my bedroom, and you're so neat and organized. Do you have a mild case of OCD?" she asked, smiling at me. My dark blue dress shirt she wore was unbuttoned, and on her tiny frame, it looked more like a dress.

I walked over to her and pulled her into me. Staring into her brightly-lit hazel eyes, I leaned down to kiss her neck. "Don't tell me you're a messy little piglet."

She snorted at that. "No! Maybe not as organized, but I'm clean."

I chuckled, then bit her ear as my hands palmed her bottom.

She moaned, begging me not to start up again.

Her scent was so inviting, a combination of my body wash and sex. "Your apartment in Tribeca," I found myself asking. "Do you live alone?"

"The apartment belongs to my brother actually. Staying there was supposed to be temporary, but he hasn't kicked me out yet. And yes, I do live there alone." She locked her arms around my neck and jumped up to straddle my waist. "You seriously need to feed me before my belly starts to sing unpleasantly."

I chuckled and slapped her bottom. "Alright. Let's go." I carried her down the stairs to the kitchen and dropped her on the island before heading to my home office. "I'll be right back"

I returned shortly to find her buttoning her shirt, *my shirt*. "I was enjoying the view."

Smiling, she took a seat behind the counter and pointed to the paper I held. "Is that a menu? What are we having?"

"No. I'm cooking for you, nothing too fancy. I hope you like baked lemon-peppered salmon," I said and slid the paper to her.

"You cook?" she looked at me in shock. "Yeah, I could eat salmon."

"Good." I turned to preheat the oven and collected the marinating salmon from the fridge. "Would you like something to drink? I have red and white wine or I can fix you something else."

"I'll have white wine please. What is this?" she asked, picking up the paper.

I grabbed a bottle of white wine, uncorked it and poured two glasses as she scanned the paper.

"Oh, it's your blood test results…from last week."

I handed her a glass and drank from mine. "I've always used a condom and get tested every few months. I thought you should know." Moving around the kitchen, I laid out the fixings for salad and grilled vegetables, and started mixing up pecans, almonds, and bread crumbs for the salmon.

"Looks like you're clean as a whistle. Great! And while we're on the subject…. weren't you sleeping with someone not too long ago, say two weeks ago, maybe more recently? Do you plan on seeing other people while…?"

"While we're fucking?" I supplied, turning to look at her and hating the way that sounded.

"Yes." She picked up her wine, swallowing half of its contents.

"No and I haven't been with anyone in over two weeks. I ended things with the person I was seeing in Pittsburgh. It was a casual thing."

Leaning her elbows on the counter, she squinted her hazels at me. "Two weeks, is that a record for you?"

"Would you like more wine?" I reupped her glass without waiting for a response.

"Are you trying to get me drunk so you can get into my pants?" she asked, smiling, her words slurring. I thought she might already be there.

I went to her and kissed her lips. "You're such a lightweight," I whispered.

"You haven't fed me." she whispered back.

"I'm working on it."

She leaned in to continue the kiss. "Work faster."

I kissed her nose and went back to the stove. "Yes ma'am."

"Your middle name is Tomás?" she asked, having read it on the test results.

"Yes. My mom grew up in the Czech Republic and was very fond of the name," I replied, the ache of my mom's memory throbbing in my chest.

"I like it," she said.

Once I had the salmon in the oven, I began grilling the vegetables as we talked about work and college years. I was quickly learning that she became more and more talkative with every sip of wine. "How come you haven't been with anyone in two years?"

Shrugging, she took another sip. "I've been busy with work, and I don't know, I just got used to not having sex, so it didn't really feel like I was not having it, you know?" she rambled.

No, I didn't know. "Sure, but I'm not complaining."

"I didn't offer to help with the cooking. That's so rude of me," she whined, taking another sip of wine. "How did you learn to cook?"

"My mother," I answered.

"Are you two very close?"

"No. She passed."

"Oh!" she gasped and nearly spilling her wine. "I'm sorry." She wiped at her lips. "About your mom."

I washed my hands and quickly dried them off with the dish cloth before moving to her. Unclasping her fingers from the wine glass, I placed it on the counter and studied her.

"Are you drunk?" I asked softly.

"Are you pissed?" She countered, straightening.

"Of course not. Why don't you hold off until you've eaten something? The salmon is almost ready," I said, cupping her face.

She nodded, staring deeply into my eyes. "Pierce, you have the most beautifulest midnight blues and they're just so...... piercing." She smiled, sliding her hands up my chest and pulling on my t-shirt.

I chuckled and pressed a kiss to her forehead. "Beautifulest?"

She nodded.

"Why do you call me Pierce?"

"Because it's your name, silly." She laughed.

"Yes, my *last* name. Although I've noticed that you like to scream *Aiden* when I'm deep inside you."

"You say the dirtiest things to me," she said in a moan, and slammed her mouth to mine, kissing me deeply. "I guess I should start getting used to calling you by your *first* name."

"You can call me which ever name you prefer. Either one sounds great on your lips."

She smiled.

The timer on the oven sounded at the same time my home phone blared in the kitchen. I walked over to the oven and turned it off before reaching for the cordless.

"Hello?" I answered.

"Mr. Pierce, it's Mack at the front desk. You have a guest, a Mr. Isaac Pierce."

Fuck!

"Alright. Please let him know I'll be down in a minute."

"He's insisting on seeing you immediately," he paused "Sir, I think he's had a drink or two," he said in a low voice.

Just what I needed right now.

"Please send him up. Thanks Mack." I disconnected the call.

I pulled the salmon out of the oven and told Christen I'd be back shortly, then headed to the foyer to meet my father.

"What are you doing here?" I barked, when the elevator doors opened.

My father stumbled out of the elevator, wearing a suit and tie with a scarf and overcoat draped over his arm, even though it about 63 degrees outside. His stocky six foot three frame was almost as tall as me. His oxfords were polished to perfection.

"Hello, son. You didn't make our lunch appointment." His reproachful tone reminded me of my childhood, and was reminiscent of the many ways my brother and I had often disappointed him.

With hands in my pockets to mirror his stance, I furrowed my brow at him. "So, you decided to show up here? How did you know where I live?"

He chuckled as if anything about this situation was funny. "You're an important man living in a city that never sleeps. Not to mention, I make it my business to know my son's whereabouts."

I remember a time when he was a very important man. Too important to be with family and especially too important to take care of them when they needed him the most. "If only you had applied the same investigative efforts when Mom and Ian needed you, perhaps they would still be here," I sneered at him, my temper simmering on the surface. "I am an adult now and my *whereabouts* are no concern of yours."

He visibly paled and threw his hands up in a helpless gesture. "Are you going to lord that over my head forever?" he yelled.

I yelled right back. "I don't need to lord it over your head because unlike you I blame myself for everything that happened. Tell me, how do *you* sleep at night?"

"I know you blame me for your brother's death and hate me for what happened to your mother, both of which I'll have to live with in regret and sadness for as long as I live and probably long after. But I have a son who is alive today, and I want nothing more than to repair my relationship with him and ask for his forgiveness."

"Because you *are* to blame. And tonight is not the time for mending fences," I snapped. "I made it very clear to you that I would be out of town and unable to make lunch. And you showing up here after you've had your bourbon fix to force my hand is not the way to go about seeking forgiveness."

The door behind me opened as Christen's sweet concerned voice echoed in the space, calming me. "Hey, is everything ok?"

My father spoke before I could respond, extending a hand to her. "Hello, I'm Isaac Pierce, Aiden's father."

Christen blushed scarlet, tugging on the front of her oversized shirt. "Hello, I'm Chris...Christen James. Nice to meet you." She smiled as she took his hand.

"I see my son's taste for stunning women has not changed," my father said as he placed a kiss to the back of her hand.

I glared at him. This interruption had gone on long enough.

"We were just about to sit for dinner, will you be join– "

"Isaac was just leaving," I cut it.

"No, my dear. Perhaps some other time."

I put a hand to Christen's lower back and moved her through the apartment door, shutting it behind us as we left my father standing in the foyer.

Chapter 19: Chris

After Aiden shut his father out and we were back in the apartment, we sat around the kitchen island and ate our meal in silence. The appetizing meal swiftly cleared away the wine coma I was falling into. The tension rolling off of Aiden was enough to give me pause. It was clear from their loud voices and Aiden's demeanor that he and his father did not get along very well. Or maybe that was an understatement.

"Are you ok?" I finally asked. When he didn't respond, I figured it was my cue to leave so he could have some privacy. I wasn't very good at dealing with my own family conflicts much less another person's, and I doubted he would open up to me about whatever his issues Isaac were, given the nature of our relationship. I use the term 'relationship' very loosely. I rolled up my sleeves and stood, taking the dishes to the sink and wiping down the countertop while Aiden sat distractedly, his thoughts elsewhere. I opted to wash the dishes by hand to give myself something to do, rather than use the dishwasher.

I was toweling off my hands when, I felt him at my back, gripping my waist as he feathered kisses to my neck. "You didn't have to do that."

I shrugged. "I wanted to and besides, you cooked, so it was only fair. The meal was delicious, by the way. Thanks for *finally* feeding me."

"Would you like dessert?" he asked, nuzzling my neck.

Hmm...I wasn't sure what kind of dessert he was offering, but said, "No, I need to get going. It's late."

His response was to pull me by the hair, causing my head to fall back for his kiss as his hardening length pressed into my lower back. "Stay. I'm not nearly finished with you."

As tempting as that sounded, I thought it best to leave. It was Sunday and I needed to get enough sleep for the workday ahead, and I was certain I wouldn't get much sleep if I stayed. There was also the part of me that refused to get used to the feelings I had when I was around him. Spending the night would do little to help with that.

"Can't. I need to get some sleep. I have an 8 a.m. call in the morning," I whispered unconvincingly, his kisses making my knees weak.

"I need to be deep inside you, but I promise to allow you at least five hours of sleep."

Sold! I nodded.

He chuckled and lifted me in his arms, carrying me up the stairs to his bedroom. The last of my nonexistent resistance dissolved when he placed me at the center of the bed and began to strip us both of clothing. When he joined me, I pushed him to his back, climbed on and slowly rode us to orgasm before we slumbered the night away.

Chapter 20: Aiden

My crazy week rolled on in its usual blur of interviews and meetings, and with the merger now finalized, I could redirect my focus to the pre-launch of our latest video game console, iAnCave 5.0. The iAnCave was one of the first games I developed while at Berkeley and it was my proudest creation. The portable game console was designed as an on-the-go gaming device to include special functions and features my brother Ian found lacking in the games we'd played as kids. Over the years, the iAnCave was redesigned to meet the demands of innovative technologies as well as consumers' wants and needs. The newest model not only allowed users to connect on any game platform from cloud gaming to mobile devices, but users could also pause a game on one device and continue on another. I was involved with every aspect of iAnCave since its conception, from development to design and marketing, and after five models, that hadn't changed. What had started off as a simple creation in honor of Ian and his love for video games, later became and still remained PGE's bestselling portable game console.

The only silver lining in my crazy week was the all too brief moments spent with Christen as she prepped me for media interviews. We hadn't spent any personal time together since Monday when I managed to convince her to spend another night at my place, despite the very busy day we had and a 7 a.m. meeting the following morning. And three days later, it was becoming clear to me that the more time I spent with her, the hungrier I got, and I knew wouldn't be satiated anytime soon. The hunger was so overwhelming, it had my balls in a constant state of blue. I should have been grateful that my work schedule left me with little time to carve out for her, this had always come in handy in the past, but now it only served to piss me off. I had plans with Lucas later, for our usual Thursday tonight catchup and would be flying to Seattle on Sunday for the Video Gamers' convention, which left Friday and hopefully Saturday nights to spend with her.

I checked my calendar and saw I had no calls or meetings scheduled for the next 57 minutes. Unable to stop myself, I sent Christen a text.

[5:03pm] Me: I need to see you in my office. Now.

Her response came a moment later.

[5:09pm] Christen: Hey, my call with the Post is running over, should be wrapping up shortly. Is   everything ok?

[5:09pm] Me: No. Come by when you're finished and leave your panties behind.

[5:10pm] Christen:

Her eyeroll emoji had me chuckling.

Twenty minutes later, there was a knock on my office door right before Christen walked in. I smiled to myself. She always knocked, but never waited for a response before entering.

"Lock the door please," I said, loud enough for her to hear from across the room.

I ended the call I was on with my realtor and moved around the desk to lean against it, watching as she strode towards me. She was elegant and sexy in a way that was effortless, making me want to dirty her up and free her body of all clothing. I wrapped an arm around her waist when she reached me and hauled her between my legs.

"What took you so long?" I leaned in to inhale her sweet scent, sliding my hands down to palm her bottom. The feel of it never failed to get me going.

She stretched on tip toes to wrap her arms around my neck, pressing her swollen breasts into my chest. "Hi," her voice was a soft whisper in my ear. "Sorry. I had an urgent call come in."

I kneaded her bottom and sucked on her neck, desperately needing to feel her tight slippery warmth clutching me. "I need to fuck you." I pulled on her bottom lip. "Why do you have panties on?"

"We can't," she said with a hint of regret.

I pulled back to look at her. "What's wrong?"

She stared at my chest, not meeting my gaze. "I have good news and bad news."

"Ok." I prompted.

"I got my period," she said, her hands moving up and down on my chest. "And I started birth control."

Both sounded like good news to me, *great* in fact. I was thankful the broken condom hadn't come back to haunt us. "Ok. So, what's the bad news?"

Her eyes met mine. "Hello...? My *period*," she said, gesturing between the small gap that separated us as she continued. "That means we can't do...anything."

I raised a brow. "Not necessarily..."

"You know what I mean."

"I'll give you today off. Tomorrow night I'm having you no matter what's happening down there."

She laughed. "How about a little something to tide you over?" she said, taking my hand and pulling me around the desk. "Sit."

I obeyed her command and drew her in for a kiss. "We don't have a lot of time, I have a meeting in 22 minutes."

She hands fell to my belt and started unbuckling as she bent to her knees, her mischievous gaze never leaving me. "Then I better start sucking."

I groaned and threw my head back against the chair, shifting in my seat to grant her better access. She tugged on my boxer briefs to release my cock, and slid her tongue from root to tip. She sucked hard on the tip before engulfing me in a heat so sweet I nearly spilled right then.

"*Fuck* baby, not so fast," I leaned forward and pulled at her hair. "Slow down," Her mouth was relentless, sucking hard as she took me down her throat. My hips rose to meet her demanding pulls. *Fuck*. I wasn't ready. It felt too damn good. Pulling back, she swirled her tongue around the head for a few seconds before deep throating me once more. She wasn't slowing down. Reaching around her, I dragged her top over her breasts and yanked down her bra. Her moans vibrated around my cock when I pinched her nipples. She had me by the balls in every way.

"You are so fucking beautiful." I uttered through the blissful agony and pulled back to release my cock from the tight grip of her mouth. "Wrap those gorgeous tits around me," I ordered harshly and watched as she cupped her heavy breasts, squeezing the taut globes around my cock, and sliding them up and down the length. My eyes were glued to the erotic sight of her tongue darting out to lick the precum seeping from the tip as I began to thrust.

"Fuck baby. Do you want my come on your pretty tits or down your throat?"

The ringing of my office line cut off whatever she was going to say. I turned and clumsily reached to send the call to voicemail, but instead hit the speaker button.

"Hello," came Lucas' voice.

"*Fuck*," I mumbled under my breath.

"What was that?" he asked.

"What do you want?" I barked.

"What the fuck is eating you?" he snapped.

Christen giggled softly around my cock and I tried to stifle a groan.

"Are you ok? You sound like you're having a heart attack."

"I'm fine," I said through gritted teeth. The suctioning of her sweet mouth readying to pull me under.

"Hey, so I'm thinking we try Haywire tonight. Klaire says it's a decent bar. We should give it a try, because if we end up at another one of those sleazy bars where the girls are begging to blow us in the bathroom, I'm gonna be pissed. I know it's been awhile since you lived in the city, but that's no excuse. You need to up your game and start taking me to better places."

Was he fucking kidding me? He thought now was the time for his inner monologue? And I didn't even want to think about the part of his tirade that had Christen briefly pausing on my cock. She began sucking in earnest again as I tuned Lucas out, my hips meeting every pull.

"Are you there? We have the Ops call in four minutes. I'm coming over."

Silence. Finally. Why hadn't I just hung up on him?

"*Fuck!* I'm coming." On a loud groan, I tensed and started pouring down her throat. Suddenly, I was pulling out of her mouth and fisting my cock to spill the rest of my come on her breasts. "Your greedy mouth needs to share," I scolded.

She glared at me with amusement in her eyes.

"Will that tide you over or do you think you'll need another blowjob at your sleazy bar tonight?" She smiled, rising to her feet and covering herself up.

I adjusted my pants, tucking in my shirt and buckling up. "Fucking Lucas," I grumbled. When she turned to move away, I reached for her and pulled her to me. "You better not think about wiping my come off. I want you smelling of me all night."

Her smile was derisive. "Yeah, sure. I'll be lying in bed tonight smelling of you while you're at the bar getting offers for blow jobs."

"Don't be ridiculous," I sneered, my gaze dropping to her breasts. "You'll lay in bed touching yourself while you wait for me."

The knock on the door startled her. She jerked away and disappeared into my private bathroom.

I walked over to the door to unlock it. Swinging it open, I scowled at Lucas who staring at me suspiciously.

"Glad to see you're alive and not having a heart attack like I'd suspected." My office phone started to ring as he strode past me.

I assumed it was the Pittsburgh office calling in for our meeting. "Can you please get that? I'll join in a minute," I said to Lucas who nodded.

I entered the bathroom to find Christen at the mirror fixing her hair, her clothes back in order. Moving to her, I spun her around to face me and leaned down to kiss her hard on the mouth. I pulled her lip into my mouth and sucked. "Is my come still on you?"

"Yes," she whispered.

"Good girl. I'm coming to your apartment after the bar. Answer your phone when I call."

"Aiden," she started.

"Yes, I know. Your period. We'll cuddle."

She bit her lip to suppress a smile and I pressed a quick kiss to it before letting her go. "Answer your phone," I repeated and followed as she left the bathroom.

I watched as she exited my office, shutting the door behind her before I joined Lucas on the conference call.

CHAPTER 21: AIDEN

"MY REALTOR CALLED WITH SOME GOOD news. The apartment in Pittsburgh sold," I said to Lucas. We were seated at the bar Klaire had recommended and so far, it was already better than the ones we normally ended up in. The traditional bar had a modern style that was warm and inviting, and the turnout wasn't bad either. The patrons threw back their drinks, enjoying the music and lively atmosphere.

"That was fast. Mine's still in escrow, but should be closing next week."

I took a pull from my beer, once again thankful that Lucas had decided to make the move to New York with me. When I was contemplating a relocation to the city eight months ago, I had brought up the idea of him coming along, knowing it was a long shot. Lucas was a Pittsburgh native with family he didn't wanted to leave behind and a mother who was recovering from a stroke. I knew I was asking a lot from him and ultimately, it was his decision to make. So I was surprised and thrilled when he agreed to come along for the ride. There are some people who might call him a selfish bastard, but these were people who didn't know him very well and maybe not at all.

Lucas and I met 11 years ago at Wharton while completing our MBA program. A short time after, he joined the small PGE team and became instrumental to the company's success. His invaluable friendship over the years had kept me grounded and on occasion, saved me from going insane.

"Thanks again for doing this," I said.

He nodded, knowing exactly what I meant. "I wanted this too you know? I think I even needed it," he said, draining the last of his beer. "As long as you stop taking me to shitty bars, we shouldn't have a problem."

I chuckled. "Looks like you won't be needing my services anymore."

"Would you boys like another round?" The blonde bartender who'd been giving Lucas flirtatious looks interrupted and quickly turned away when we nodded.

"What's that supposed to mean?" he asked.

"I believe you're taking recommendations from *Klaire* with a K now," I said. "I'm sure you can ask her for other suggestions. And while we're on the subject, is there anything going on between the two of you I should know about?" I immediately regretted the words as I spoke them.

He snorted and made a dramatic show of turning to face me, his brow raised. "Anything going on between *us*? *Really*?" he asked with an emphasis at the end of each question. "Do you mean are we doing only God-knows-what in my office while I'm on the phone and then sneaking her out of bathroom afterwards?" He finished with a sly grin.

No one ever accused him of being a fool. "You've made your point, now shut up."

"The answer would be a no. Klaire with a K and I are doing no such thing. She's not even my type and I have zero interest in blurring those lines."

"I take it you saw Christen leaving my office?"

"Yes, I did see Christen with a *C* leaving your office, seeing as how my 20/20 vision was still intact the last time I checked. I think Klaire and your girl should trade letters."

I took a pull from the beer the bartender placed in front of me to suppress my answering chuckle.

"I suspect she'll be your plus one for the gala? Clearly, things have progressed between you two, against all advice."

"Let's not get ahead of ourselves. Yes things have progressed between us, but the Wishing on a Game gala is what? Three months away?"

"Sure, but we'll need to RSVP in a week or two."

I ignored that line of reasoning. "What do you mean Klaire is not your type?"

He shrugged. "Sure, she's hot, but she's a little too out-spoken and abrasive. I like to be the one in charge and in control, and apparently, so does she."

Molly, the bartender checked in again for what seemed like the tenth time in the last five minutes, despite the crowded bar and others vying for her attention. "So, you have thought about it?"

"Not exactly. She has a boyfriend, so that point is moot. Not to mention for all the other reasons."

"Since when has that stopped you?"

He turned to look at me. "Remember Trishelle?"

The look on my face said I'd rather not. "*Ooo, yeah.*"

"*Exactly.*"

I nodded. "Good point."

"We may have a friendly conversation here and there, but there's nothing more to it. I'm not interested."

"Got it," I said, surrendering.

The music blared and the crowd grew louder as we chatted about the new iAnCave launch and the Wishing on a Game gala that PGE had been a proud supporter and sponsor of the past four years. The gala usually held at the Astoria was a charity event that raised money through ticket sales, live auctions, video games and other charitable donations for various children hospitals all around the country.

When Molly stopped to check in on us again, we both ordered two fingers of Jameson before I headed to the restroom. Returning, I took a swig of my drink. The music seemed to have gotten louder, and with every new addition to the crowd came less air to breathe in. I loosened the knot of my tie to abate the stifling air and pulled out my phone to text Christen.

[9:37pm] Me: Are you up? I'll be there in 30.

I pocketed my phone and looked up to find two attractive women talking to Lucas, one of them eyeing me like a starving kitten as Lucas made introductions.

Jeez, he worked fast.

The eyeing blonde reached out a hand. "Hi. Melissa."

"Hello. Aiden," I replied, taking her hand for a quick shake before releasing it as her eyes raked over me.

"I'm Shanna, nice to meet you." the second blonde said, clinging to Lucas and offering up her hand.

I took it in mine. "Likewise."

"What do you do, handsome?" Melissa asked, licking her lips in a manner that was anything but seductive or even attractive.

"I play video games."

Her lips parted to speak, pausing as if confused, then asked, "For a living? That must be fun."

"It is," I said, pulling out my phone and checking for a response from Christen. Nothing yet.

"Maybe we can play sometime?" she suggested, leaning in and placing a hand on my arm. "Or tonight if you're available."

I wasn't interested and not just because I was in a hurry to see Christen, although that was a big reason. She was too forward and her approach reeked of desperation. "I'm not," I said.

"Would you guys like to get out of here and maybe go somewhere more private?" Shanna interrupted, obviously not having heard our conversation.

"I'm headed out to meet someone. Sorry." I wasn't sorry. The sound from my phone alerted me to a text, which I swiped through to read, then sent a reply.

> [9:45pm] CHRISTEN: Yes, but not for much longer. My apt# is 2611, building code is: *97842#

> [9:46pm] Me: On my way babe.

"I gotta go, man. We'll discuss Seattle tomorrow," I said to Lucas before addressing the blondes. "Nice meeting you ladies."

"Bye." The girls singsonged in unison.

"Say hello to Christen for me." Lucas said.

I left the bar and flagged down a taxi.

Chapter 22: Chris

When I heard the knock, I immediately jumped out of my bed, pulled on a satin robe and practically ran to the door. The sleep that was tempting me away, vanished completely. And I needed the sleep after my tiresome day, but I needed him more. Reaching the door, I checked the peephole before unlocking it and pulled it opened.

"Hey," I greeted, fighting the urge to jump on him. He looked even more delicious than he had earlier. His tie was loosened, shirt sleeves rolled up and his overgrown hair that was in serious need of a cut was messily tousled with a few strands falling over his eyes.

A long sensuous kiss was his response as he stepped in and draw me to him, the door shutting behind him. The intimate gliding of his tongue combined with the heady taste of potent liquor was arousing, instantly making me dizzy.

"Where's the bedroom?" he asked, picking me up.

I straddled his waist. "Down over there." I mumbled into his neck, breathing in his intoxicating scent.

His deep chuckled caused me to shiver. "Thanks. That's very helpful." He said, but located my bedroom easily, shutting the door behind us and laying me gently unto the queen-sized bed. Sitting up, I shrugged off my robe and watched him disrobed. His dark blue eyes roamed over me, taking in my short shorts and lingering for long moments on the thin tank top that outlined my breasts.

"You remember we can't. Right?" I whispered when he climbed over me.

"I remember," he kissed along my neck. "However, I never promised to keep my hands to myself."

We made out for a while before reluctantly pulling apart to get under the covers. I lay snuggled against his back, moaning as his hands massaged my aching breasts.

"I want you here," he said, pressing his groin into my ass.

I laughed nervously. "I don't think so."

"I don't mean tonight, but I will have you there." He pressed into my neck, kissing me hotly. The abrasion of his beard sent shivers down my spine, even as the heat from his body seeped into me. "We have all weekend for that. Now go to sleep."

Too exhausted to argue, I snuggled in closer and obeyed.

A couple hours before my alarm was scheduled to go off, I felt Aiden shuffling about restlessly. He was whispering the now familiar words I had heard twice before when we spent nights together.

I'm sorry, Mom. I'm so sorry.

I moved closer to him, sliding a hand up and down his arm. "It's okay, baby," I whispered to him. This seemed to help like the other times I had done so, because he was silent again. I continued the soothing motion, unable to fall back asleep. An hour later I turned off the alarm so it wouldn't go off and headed to the bathroom for a shower. When I returned to the bedroom, Aiden was sitting at the edge of the bed. His elbows rested on his knees as he raked his hands through his hair.

"Hey," I said, fastening the ties of my bathrobe. I moved to stand between his legs and pulled on his wrists, replacing his hands with mine and gently massaged his scalp. "You ok?"

He lifted his head and pulled me closer, untying my robe and placing kisses along my stomach. "You're spending the weekend in my bed."

"Did you sleep ok?" I asked.

Again, he ignored my question. "You're going to have to take another shower. I want to watch my cock disappearing into your mouth before I take you against the wall. Next time, you'll wait for me. And I don't give a damn about the period."

With that he hauled me over his shoulder and headed to the bathroom.

Chapter 23: Chris

I ARRIVED WORK EARLIER THAN EXPECTED and made a beeline for the gym. I felt energized, and with plenty of time to spare before my first meeting, I couldn't think of a better way to expel some of that energy. Considering the mind-blowing session in the shower with Aiden earlier, I shouldn't have been so hyper. Afterwards, he had taken a cab home to change as I headed into work. The things he did to my body were unreal and threw me off guard. My emotions were all over the place, and trying to reel them in got me nowhere. I was developing non-casual-sex feelings for him and he was all to blame. He cooked for me, was at times very tender and loving in the way he held me closely after our marathon sexcapades, and was great company. We were spending more than a normal amount of personal time together for two people who were *casually* seeing one another. Although, we spent most of that time in bed, where he was either fucking me hard or tenderly moving into me like I was the most precious thing he'd ever held, while he groaned out the filthiest things. We didn't talk about our families or discuss much about other aspects of our personal lives, but the connection we shared was too intense to dismiss so easily.

This morning, I'd wanted to broach the subject of him talking in his sleep, but thought it wasn't the right time, so I'd dismissed it just like the other times. There was the possibility that he may not want to talk to me about whatever was bothering him, or maybe I wasn't ready to bring it up. Besides I didn't think we had that kind of relationship anyway. So, I would mind my business when it came to family matters.

I increased the speed on the treadmill and ran faster, thinking of the day ahead while making mental notes of tasks to complete and calls to return, which reminded me of my brother's missed call earlier in the week. With work on full throttle this week and my budding *casualship* with Aiden, the call had selfishly slipped my mind. I'd also meant to text Klaire last night about her Haywire recommendation to Lucas, the same Lucas she thought of as rude. I ran for five more miles, then stepped off to hit the showers, my third this morning.

Later that afternoon, I returned to my office following a few offsite meetings – one of which was a late lunch meeting with Aiden, Lucas, and Game World Today magazine to discuss the new iAnCave launch. As Aiden and Lucas discussed the game's history and the changes to iAnCave over the years, I listened intently, not having known the inspiration behind the game. Aiden very briefly touched on his brother's love for video games, and hearing him speak in the past tense momentarily gave me pause, but before I could process it, he had moved on to design and product placement. I had read everything I could find online regarding PGE, before and during the merger. And once I'd met its elusive CEO, I read up on anything I could find concerning him. Since Aiden didn't speak about his personal life, I was limited to the Internet, which listed almost nothing on that front. I didn't know he had a brother, and when Aiden had implied he was no longer alive, I wondered if I'd heard him correctly. Could that be the source of tension between Aiden and his father, and why he asked for his mother's forgiveness in his sleep? I was pondering these questions and had been lost in thought when I missed the one that was directed at me from Peter, the magazine's head writer. I redirected my attention to find several pairs of eyes focused on me. I gave a small laugh and asked the question be repeated, then proceeded to seamlessly transition the conversation into talks of announcements, coverage, and content marketing. I hadn't missed the questioning look Aiden had given me.

Back at my office, I plopped down in my chair to relieve my tired feet from all the walking around in the city while in my Choos. I dug into my purse for my phone, ready to shoot Klaire a text, when I noticed a couple from Aiden.

[3:12pm] Aiden: What was that about?

I sent a reply, opting to go with ignorance.

[3:22pm] Me: What was what about?

I sent Klaire a text and reached for my office phone to return David's call. When he didn't answer, I left a voicemail. I was unlocking my computer when my cell pinged with a text at the same time my office phone started ringing. I took the call with David as I read the text from Aiden on my cell.

> [3:29pm] Aiden: I'm in meetings till 5:30. Do you want to ride home with me afterwards or do you need to go to your place first?

I dropped my cell so that I could pay attention to David. We caught up for the next 20 minutes or so about his work, my work, our parents, our brother Matthew's visit in a few weeks, and the upcoming Sunday dinner that we would both be present for. We were finalizing a lunch meeting for next week when there was a knock on my door before Klaire walked in. I raised a hand to signal I'd be just a minute. Ending the call, I typed a reply to Aiden, saying I'd need to go home first and would take a cab to his place afterwards.

Klaire cleared her throat. "Are you about done yet and what's with the lovey dovey smile?" She teased in a silly country accent.

My smile widened. "Just about." I returned in my own silly country accent.

She lifted her cell phone, indicting my earlier text to her. "What's with the 'you have some explaining to do' text? What exactly am I explaining?"

Yes. About *that*. "I hear you and Lucas are…getting a little chummy." My statement sounded more like a question.

She arched a brow and folded her arms. "You want to run that by me again?"

I sighed, feeling foolish. "Nothing. Forget I said anything."

"Oh no, please do elaborate," she pressed.

"Haywire," I said simply.

She laughed, a little too hard. "I'm getting chummy with Lucas because of a bar suggestion?"

I narrowed suspicious eyes at her. "It wasn't just any bar suggestion," I accused. "We discovered that place and you shared it with another so freely. And with someone you've said is so rude no less?" My accusation might not have made a lot of sense at first, but the more I thought about it, the more it began to make perfect sense. Bar hopping could be tedious, so when we'd found this gem of a bar, we vowed it would be our secret spot and sharing said secret spot, with a 'rude' someone didn't exactly add up.

She rolled her eyes. "Whatever."

I pointed at her. "I see you Klaire."

"It was an accident, ok," she snapped defensively. "We were discussing language for some internal memo when he rudely took a personal call, right in the middle of our conversation!" She leaned forward, a look of disgust apparent in her features. "And I overhead him saying, *to probably some non-sleazy chick,* that 'the bars in the city are *sleazy*'. I took offense to that. So when he ended the call, I found myself telling him about Haywire. I have no idea how it happened. I'm sorry, I had to defend our city."

It was my turn to laugh. "Fine, you're forgiven. Did you at least find out if he liked it?"

"I don't care if he liked it or not." Her expression was one of horror. "I wish I'd sent him to a gross strip club instead."

"Ah Uh. Ok." I said. "How do you like working with him? Personally, I think he's very precise and exacting. He and Aiden seem to have a lot in common, it's kind of eerie. Their approach to business is direct, authoritative and concise. And they never talk about their personal lives, not even in casual conversation. What do you think?"

Klaire straightened in her seat. "Well let's see, I think he's arrogant, self-centered, indifferent, flippant, and rude," she said without missing a beat.

Smiling, I asked, "Are you attracted to him?"

"Are you seriously asking me that? Why would I be?" she scoffed haughtily.

I shrugged. "You did say he was attractive the first time you met him, if I remember correctly."

"That was weeks ago. And just because I think he is attractive does not mean *I am* attracted to him," she sighed. "How are things with you and Aiden? Was he the one on the phone or the one you were texting?"

As if on cue, my text alert sounded. I ignored it. "Great! Everything's great. How are things with you? How's your dad?" I asked, shifting gears.

"My stepmom's a bitch, my stepbrother is an ass, dad's still dying, and I'm just dandy."

"You're in a mood. Wish I had some wine to serve you with all that whining." I teased.

"You asked," she said in a whiny voice.

"You do realize that Alice and your dad aren't married? So, they're not exactly your *step* anything."

"I don't know what else to call them – this is easier." she said, pushing to her feet. "What do you and Aiden have planned for the weekend?"

I shrugged, aiming for nonchalance. "Nothing really, just hanging out I guess."

"Hmm," she said. "Alrighty then, later!"

"Later." I returned as she left my office.

Chapter 24: Chris

Aiden and I lay sprawled out on his living room floor, my breathing still heavy from our fast and furious mating of only moments ago. I stared out the sliding glass doors that led out into the terrace, wondering if it would always be this good, this urgent, this desperate. Returning home after work, I showered and packed a small overnight bag for our weekend together. No sooner had I stepped through his apartment door when he pulled me to him. We were at each other like sex starved nymphos and I wasn't the least bit embarrassed. I craved his desire and the unapologetic need that consumed him, which only fueled my desperation.

I turned back to Aiden and maneuvered myself so that I was fully on top of him. "We have got to stop meeting like this," I teased, placing kisses along his jaw and enjoying the feel of his scruff against my skin. I shrieked when he flipped me to my back, his muscled body weighing me down.

He pulled my arms over my head and pinned my wrists to the area rug. "I'm sorry. You turn me into an animal," his expression conveyed anything but remorse.

"Are you hungry?" he asked, flexing his hips against my sex.

I let out a small moan. "I'm always hungry for you."

His look turned salacious as the pressure on my wrists intensified. "I meant for food."

I sighed contentedly. "Then why are you wet-humping me? But yes, I could eat." The weight of his body felt so good, so I was in no hurry to get up.

"Come on," he said, pulling me up with him. "We have dinner reservations."

"We do?" I asked, surprised as I bent to pick up my discarded clothing from the sparsely carpeted and yet-to-be furnished living room floor.

"Yes. I'm feeding you Mediterranean tonight." He stood gloriously naked and unaware of the heat beginning to creep its way up my neck.

I tried not to ogle the beautiful symmetry that was his masculine and very virile form as he moved around the room, picking up his clothes and righting some vinyl records by a corner wall that must have been knocked askew in his haste to get inside me. Apparently, he was a beastly animal in business and in bed with a penchant for meticulous order as I mused distractedly, the sight of him tempted me to demand he take me again. I was fumbling to right my top when he reached for my hand and pulled me towards the stairs.

"Don't bother with the top. I like this view just fine, in fact, I'd prefer it if you were always naked whenever you're here."

And I'd prefer it if you did the same, I thought, before shooting him a dirty look.

He chuckled. "Since I'm a fair man, I'd settle for you being topless."

"You still haven't furnished or decorated your apartment," I stated lamely, not wanting to think about how nice it was spending time with him, here or anywhere else.

"Actually, I'm expecting a delivery tomorrow. I've had to reschedule a few. Are you offering me your services?"

"Oh," was all I could manage before he lifted me and took me up the stairs.

CHAPTER 25: CHRIS

WE ARRIVED AT THE BUSY AND nearly packed restaurant an hour past our reservation time, but we were immediately escorted by a tall and friendly hostess who greeted Aiden by name the moment we walked in. Our shower had run long and I almost felt guilty over the excess water we used while Aiden had insisted on doing dirty things to my body. *Almost*.

Opting to take an Uber, Aiden and I had made out in the back seat of the SUV with me practically in his lap and his hands up my short dress the entire ride. Everything about this man intrigued me and apparently brought out the naughty high school slut I had never been. His brooding demeanor and formidable exterior no longer intimidated, because sometimes I got a glimpse of a softer side, a playful side and I wanted every side. At just the thought of the way he fucked me with consummate passion and fierceness was enough to summon the butterflies. I felt sexually sated and relaxed, and not even the all too friendly smiles directed at Aiden from the hostess, who was determined to deny my existence, could dampen the sexual high I was on. Because at the end of the night, it was my thighs he was going to be between.

The restaurant was both elegant and casually understated from its high ceiling chandeliers to the mix of fine dining and cozy U-shaped booth seating. We were led to a booth towards the back of the restaurant, the semi-private area affording us some quiet, along with a nice window view. Our server came moments later to take our drink orders of pomegranate prosecco for me and bourbon for Aiden, after which I excused myself to go to the restroom. I finger combed my messy waves falling down my back as best as I could and pulled at the long sleeves of my short navy dress. The dress was simple and casual, but the somewhat revealing neckline of the stretchy fitted fabric, combined with my low heels, made it appear less so. Watching Aiden as I approached the booth, my suddenly weakened knees started to wobble. He was almost a foot taller than my five foot six height, wearing dark blue denims that molded to his powerful legs and a black dress shirt tucked halfway in, revealing his low riding belt buckle. I had been too preoccupied in my sex haze to fully take him in earlier. His messy hair – no doubt my doing in the car – was pulled back and curled behind his ears. I wanted to hop on his roller coaster and grab on for dear life. As if I had spoken that wicked thought out loud, he stretched an arm out for me, almost instinctively before his gaze shifted to me and I moved into his arm as he pulled me closer. It was then that I noticed he was in conversation with an older gentleman.

"Christen, this is Andreas," Aiden said, introducing me to the older man who looked to be in his early sixties.

"Good evening, how are you?" I asked, both his calloused hands swallowing my offered one. The man was also tall with a slight build and kind expressive hazel eyes that drew a smile from me.

"Wonderful, yes? Beautiful girl in my restaurant. I am happy, no?" he said, or asked, in what could have been a Greek accent, I wasn't sure, but my smile widened.

Andreas proceeded to flirt. His accent which hadn't been so strong at first sounded a bit exaggerated for my benefit. I laughed while Aiden glared.

"Aren't you needed in the kitchen?" Aiden asked rudely, his hand at my waist sliding dangerously close to my bottom.

"Ah, yes," he replied, not looking away from me. "Christen, you must come again. I have known Aiden since he was a small boy and he never bring his woman to my restaurant."

I almost snorted, not sure if it was at the term 'woman' or him assuming I was Aiden's *woman*. I covered my almost snort with a laugh instead as he spoke again.

"So always, your food is on the house." He took my hand again in both of his and squeezed, his wedding band feeling cool against my skin. "Very nice meeting you, beautiful Christen."

I beamed at him. "Thank you. The pleasure was mine."

He lifted his head pointedly at Aiden. "Talk to your father. In this life, family is everything." All traces of the jovial Andreas, disappeared. Aiden stiffened and the hand sliding a path to my bottom briefly stilled.

Andreas sighed. "Your meal is not on the house tonight," he said in jest.

Aiden turned to sit, pulling me with him to do the same. A weird silence followed before Andreas spoke again, telling me he'd be sending out small plates of the restaurant's specials for me to sample.

I smiled and thanked him.

He started to leave, but paused in step. "Christen, you take care of this man, ok?"

Ah…. ok. "I'll try," I said.

He nodded and turned to leave.

I took a sip of my now lukewarm drink, but before I could take another, the server appeared with a freshly made one to replace it. I could only assume Andreas had sent him. I glanced at Aiden who was staring straight ahead, a glass of off the rocks bourbon at his lips. We were sitting so close our thighs touched, his legs wide apart and an arm draped around the back of my seat. Yet somehow, he felt far away. This father subject always seemed to rear its ugly head like a dark cloud and usually when we were about to eat.

"We should order," I said, breaking the silence.

"I've ordered for us." He said.

Ok, I hope that wasn't all I was going to get, because I was not letting him off that easy. I had quite a few questions, but I was going to start small. "Andreas is a family friend?"

"You could say that."

"He seems to care for you," I said, placing a soothing hand on his thigh.

He placed the bourbon on the table and drank from his water. "I gave him advice on stock investments some years ago that paid off. He's grateful for that otherwise he probably wouldn't be speaking to me."

"Why is that?"

He looked at me then. "Because he's aware of the issues my father and I have and he blames me."

"What *are* these issues?" I whispered, not wanting to overstep my bounds. He had daddy issues, Klaire had daddy issues. Was I the only one without them?

"My mom's death," he paused, taking another drink of water. "Among other things."

That was not what I was expecting to hear. His mother died and he blames his dad? Why? Would it be prying to ask? I mean, he did sort of bring it up. Which reminded me of something he had said during our meeting with Game World Today magazine, something about his brother.

"Aiden...." I began, but stopped when the server interrupted my thoughts to dish out our meal. The delicious smells wafting from the plates stirred my hunger back to life and were almost enough to distract me from my curious thoughts. Aiden sliced into the lamb shish kabob while I sampled the grilled chicken and tabouli salad. I nearly sighed when the intense flavors hit my tongue. We ate in silence for several minutes as plate after plate was served, just as Andreas had promised.

"You're into the stock market?" I asked.

"I dabble here and there."

I didn't know much about stock trading or investing in stocks or what have you, but my brothers did and whenever I had questions, I deferred to them. "Aren't there a lot of risks involved?"

"There are risks involved with just about anything," he said, chuckling and cocked his head at me. "Some risks are worth taking.... and so sweet when they pay off."

I swallowed and licked my lips, momentarily forgetting what we were talking about.

"Do you gamble?" he asked.

"What kind of gambling?" Like with one's heart? I thought to myself.

"Like poker? Do you play?"

Right, of course. "No, some roulette, maybe blackjack."

"I'll have to teach you then."

"I'm sorry to hear about your mother." I blurted out of nowhere and felt terrible when his fork stopped short of his lips. When he mentioned her last week, I had been drinking on an empty stomach and didn't want to say the wrong thing. I wanted to know more, but was afraid her would retreat. "When did she pass?" I heard myself asking.

"Two years ago." was all he offered.

The server returned to ask if we wanted dessert. Aiden looked to me to answer, I shook my head and asked for another drink instead.

"Yes, absolutely." The server said before clearing away the empty plates.

Returning to our conversation, I asked, "Was she sick?" For a moment, he said nothing and I thought he wasn't going to respond, but then he did.

"It was a car accident. We later found out that her blood alcohol level had been well over the limit."

"Oh. I'm so sorry," I managed to say in a crocked whisper.

Aiden stood suddenly, looking completely unfazed. "I'm going to the restroom. I'll be right back. Do you want anything else?"

I wasn't sure if he meant to food or answers. I shook my head and watched as he walked away, effectively putting an end to the conversation. I picked up the drink the server brought and downed half its contents as I nodded for the remaining dishes to be cleared. When I asked for the check, he said, "It's been care of."

I sat for what felt like an hour, waiting for Aiden, and when he still hadn't returned, I got up to search for him. I grabbed the light sports coat he had come in with and left a couple bills on the table. Did he leave? Was he so upset that he couldn't take me home? I was walking past the restrooms when I spotted him talking to a woman with jet black hair. Oh great! It was the overly-friendly hostess who had been making a meal of him with her eyes when we'd first walked in. I reached into my purse for my phone to request an Uber, before making my way to them.

"Hey! There you are. I thought you left," I said to Aiden and could have sworn I heard the hostess choke down an involuntary laugh.

He raised a brow. "Left without you? Why would I do that?" He looked both angry and perplexed.

I shrugged. Smiling, I turned to face the hostess. "Hi. I'm Chris." I said, and not at all in a bitchy or sarcastic way. I never played games when it came to other women, and at 28, I was yet to acquire a taste for cattiness. All that was unnecessary. A man either wanted you or he didn't, and if it was the latter, I don't think the *other* woman should be to blame.

"Hi. Nice meeting you," were her words, but her eyes communicated otherwise, and I noticed she hadn't offered up a name.

"This is Amelia. She's Andreas's daughter," Aiden supplied.

She was tall, just like her dad and in five-inch heels, she was almost as tall as Aiden. I suddenly felt very short with my two-inch heels barely adding anything to my height. "Oh. Your dad is a lovely man. Please give our thanks for the wonderful meal."

She gave what resembled a fake smile. "Sure."

"You ready?" Aiden reached for the coat I was holding and wrapped a hand low around waist, cupping my hip.

"Yes." I said, taking a handful of mints from the hostess stand.

"Amelia." Aiden said by way of goodbye as he steered me towards the exist.

"I called an Uber," I said once we were outside, checking my phone for the driver's ETA when Aiden pulled me against his hard body.

Leaning beside the wall across from the valet stand, he positioned me between his legs, my back to the street as honking cars sped by. "Yeah? Around the same time you had decided I left you behind?"

"I didn't *decide*, I *thought* you left," I replied, holding onto him for balance.

"Why?" he grunted.

"I thought you were upset about… you know, about me bringing up your mom."

"I wasn't and I believe I brought her up. Even if I were upset, you think I would leave you at a restaurant or anywhere else?"

I shrugged. "Did you used to date the hostess?" My aptitude for randomly jumping from one topic to another was truly a gift – one I had perfected over the years.

"What?" He asked, sounding baffled.

I didn't relent. "Did you sleep with her?" For some reason, I couldn't meet his gaze. "It's no big deal, I'm just curious." Said the liar. I was definitely a little more than curious.

"Oh, thanks for clarifying. Your question makes *a lot* more sense now," he said sardonically. "For Christ's sake, she's like a little sister to me."

I guess that answered my question. "I'm very certain she doesn't have brotherly feelings for *you*," I muttered under my breath, but his raised brow indicated he'd heard me. Then again, we were standing pressed to each other, so he couldn't have missed it. My phone pinged and I checked it to see that the Uber had arrived. Thank God! I needed out of this conversation stat!

"Uber's here!" I announced with glee.

He scowled at me.

"Where are we headed?" he asked once we were seated in the car.

"Your place?"

"Can you hang on a minute?" Aiden said to the driver who was moving his head to the beat of the classical rock station, but nodded. Turning back to me and he said, "I don't think that's a good idea right now."

"Umm, why?" I asked, unsure of myself.

He voice lowered when he spoke. "Because of what I want to do to you right now."

My spine tingled with apprehension and lust. "What do you want to do?" I whispered, afraid the driver would hear.

"Take you over my knee for starters."

"I should have known I wasn't getting off that easy. *Or am I?*" I asked breathily, biting my bottom lip.

He lowered his lips to my ear. "And before your ass was all nice and ready, you'll be begging to feel my cock there." He leaned in and kissed me softly. "Then hopefully, you'll know better than to ask me ridiculous questions about hostesses."

My body shivered and my head bobbled. "I'm completely amenable to your suggestion." I slurred like a perverted horn dog.

"But first, I need to calm down."

"Ok," I said, somewhat disappointed.

"Now, put in an address for the nearest movie theater and pull up your dress." He directed as he slid a hand between my thighs.

I wanted to beg him to take me now. "Ok" I said.

Chapter 26: Chris

We were walking up West 42nd Street to the movie theater when we ran into Isaac and a female companion who had an arm locked in the crook of his.

"For fuck's sake," Aiden muttered under his breath.

"Aiden!" Isaac's female companion beamed as she approached and made to give him a hug. "How lovely running into you. Your dad and I were just talking about you over dinner."

"Hello Ellen," Aiden greeted, giving her a hug and a kiss on the cheek. "How are you?"

"Very well and you're looking handsome as usual." Ellen's smile got even brighter if that were possible.

"Hello son." Isaac said in greeting.

Aiden nodded. "Father."

"Good evening, Isaac," I said with a smile.

"Chris, it's a pleasure seeing you again," Isaac said and made introductions. "This is Ellen, my partner. Ellen, Chris."

She took my outstretched hand, her warm smile still in place. "Nice to meet you."

She looked regal in white dress pants and a silk blouse with a Hermès scarf wrapped around her elegant neck. Her blonde hair was a pixie cut with long strands in the front that was secured behind her ear and away from her smooth face. The youthful style put Ellen in her late thirties, but the deep wrinkles around her eyes bespoke a much older age.

"I was telling your dad we must have you over for dinner on Sunday. We would love to catch up with you, Aiden." Ellen's voice was pleading, her gaze beseeching.

"Ellen," Isaac admonished.

She ignored him and turned to me. "You both should come."

I shifted uncomfortably, fidgeting with my unruly hair, made more so by the cool breeze. All around us, people milled about from every direction and it didn't help that we were practically blocking the flow of traffic, standing so close to the theater's entrance. "I would love to, but I have a prior engagement and Aiden will be traveling on Sunday."

Ellen's face fell, which prompted me to add, "How about some other time? In a week or two?" Oh God, did I really just say that!

Isaac made a grunting sound. "That's very kind of you Chris, but I'm sure Aiden won't be so accommodating. We are yet to reschedule our lunch."

"That sounds great. Why don't we exchange numbers?" Ellen suggested.

"We're late for our movie," Aiden said, cutting in. He apologized, then we abruptly said our goodbyes and all but dragged me along with him.

"Was that really necessary?" I huffed. "You didn't have to be so rude?"

"Don't," he said in a tone that brooked no argument.

Alrighty then.

With my hand in his, he strode to a ticketing kiosk and purchased tickets to the Captain America movie. "Do you want anything?"

"I'll have water and gummy bears," I said.

After he made the purchases, we walked into the chilly theater where Aiden handed me his sports coat and I snuggled into my seat, my thoughts a scattered mess as the movie began.

Chapter 27: Chris

We were silent for the whole movie – well I suppose due to the fact that we at the movies – and all through the cab ride back to his place. I wanted to broach the subject of his dad again, but his mood was somber with an unspoken warning that read, 'Whatever you're thinking, now is not the time,' and I was too exhausted to get into an argument. As enjoyable as the movie had been, I was lost in thought for a good portion of it. I was present on two separate occasions where I witnessed his mood completely change after interacting with Isaac, so technically it made sense that I would want to know more about their relationship and to understand the reason for the tension. I was in it now and tomorrow would come soon enough. Tonight, I wanted him to take out his frustration or anger or whatever out on my body, in the most pleasurable of ways.

Aiden led me straight to his bedroom when we got back to his place. It was past 2 a.m., but I was in the mood for whatever he was in the mood for. And he certainly didn't make me wait to find out what that was.

He proceeded to strip us of our clothing and without any words, he laid me on the bed. Slowing peeling off my panties, he leaned over my exposed sex and slowly took his time licking me there, giving my clit an expert tongue slashing as I writhed beneath his skillful ministrations.

"Let go," he rasped against my folds, his mouth sucking on me as his squeezed my bottom, hard. The pleasure was too much and not enough. I wanted him moving over me, inside me.

"Let go," he repeated.

"No." I moaned, not wanting to give in. I leaned forward to reach for him. "Come here, please. I need you inside."

A sly smile spread across his lips before he slid a thumb into my rear and plunged his tongue into me.

I let out a choked scream as I involuntarily shattered all over his lips and fingers.

"Good girl," he said, climbing over my body to take a hardened nipple into his month and sucking hard.

I fought to control my breathing even as my hand slipped into his hair to hold him to me. Torturous minutes later, he moved to the bedside table to retrieve a condom. I stared at him confused. "What are you doing? We haven't used that the last I-can't-remember how many times we've fucked and I'm on birth control now. Remember?"

He chuckled, his head falling forward to rest between my breasts. "Sorry, force of habit."

"It's ok. I rather like that it's different between–
"

He plunged into me, cutting off the last of my words and eliciting a satisfactory groan from me. Our bodies moved in complete harmony as we rotted into each other. I wondered if I would be able to feel this kind of sexual affinity with another person. Would another man be able to awaken my senses the way he did when this was over? I never thought I would have this even, so I guess anything was possible.

"You ok?"

My voice shook when I replied "Yes, more than ok." I was suddenly feeling way too emotional for my liking. I pushed against his hard chest so that he lay on his back and then I climbed over him, riding us to repletion before collapsing on top of him as sleep took over.

The following morning, I woke to the sound of Aiden's blackout shades retreating into the ceiling to reveal a perfectly blue sky. I stretched and twisted in the sheets, trying to rid my face of the ridiculous smile that kept widening as I recalled Aiden grumbling "I need to have you" into my ear two hours ago, right before he began sliding his perfect cock into me. Yes, at the moment, everything was perfect.

I sat up on the ginormous bed to find I was alone, but sensed he wasn't too far away. Getting out of bed, I walked naked to the window, taking in the magnificent view that was Manhattan – a view that never got old no matter how many times I experienced it. There wasn't a single trace of the blackout shades, which I suspected were on a timer. I laughed to myself, taking in the meticulously organized space that surrounded me as I walked to the bathroom. I washed my face and brushed my teeth with the spare Phillips brush head Aiden had given me during my first sleepover, then went in search of something to throw on. I wasn't sure where he had placed my overnight bag, so I tossed on a neatly folded t-shirt from his closet.

A thorough search of both floors hadn't revealed Aiden, but I did find my overnight bag which was exactly where I'd dropped it upon my arrival yesterday. It was approaching 9 a.m. when I turned on my phone and headed back to the bedroom, the different sounds of my phone notifications went off in rapid succession, alerting me to emails, voicemails, and text messages. There were two texts from Aiden sent 30 minutes ago, the first asking if I was awake and the second saying he was at the gym on the building's 5th floor. I wished he had woken me up. I could have used a rigorous workout after stuffing my face like a little pig last night, the Mediterranean feast had been so good and I would gladly do it again. I sent him a reply demanding he return immediately to make me breakfast and added in a smiley face. I responded to a few texts from Klaire, asking what I was up to, and although she sounded casual, I got the feeling something was up. I made a mental note to call her if she kept up the façade. I was just about done with responding to some personal and work emails, which would have taken a lot less time had I not been too lazy to retrieve my laptop from my bag, when my phone started ringing.

I swiped across the answer bar to take the call. "Hi, Mom."

"Hello, daughter. How are you? Did you get the voicemail I left you this morning?" My mom asked a little too loud, even with the chattering in the background.

"Yes mom, I saw you called, but haven't listened to your message yet. Everything ok?"

"Are you still sleeping? Christen, it is ten in the morning." She said this like I was some jobless bum, and it wasn't even 10 o' clock yet.

I sighed. "No, I am not still sleeping. And it is *Saturday*, so I think I would be entitled. What's all that noise? Where are you?"

"Hold on, dear." I heard her arguing with someone in the background about fish not being fresh enough. She must be at the farmer's market. I put the phone on speaker, knowing I'd probably be on hold for at least five minutes. My mom loved to multitask while on the phone. It was great for her, not so much for the person on the other end. I used the opportunity to read Aiden and Klaire's response to my earlier texts.

> [9:28am] Aiden: Your wish is my command. I'm grabbing a few things from the store. See you soon.

> [9:30am] Klaire: Everything's good. Just wondering if you're still at Aiden's.

I replied to Klaire's text.

> [9:41am] Me: Yeah, I think I'll be here all day. Wanna stop by?

"…. Sunday dinner?" My mom's voice came through the speaker.

"What about Sunday dinner?" I asked, having missed the first part of the question.

"Will you be there?"

"Yes Mom, I already told you I would be." The apartment's door alarm beeped, signaling an entry. Aiden must be home.

"Ok. I want to make sure something at work hasn't come up again."

Fair enough. She did have a valid point. I have used work on a few occasions as an excuse to get out of Sunday dinner. Although, most of the time it wasn't a lie.

Hearing footsteps approach on the stone staircase, I switched the call off from speaker and held it o my ear. "Yes Mom, I'll be there. Give dad a kiss for me. I'll talk to you later." I said hastily, attempting to end the conversation as I paced the bedroom floor.

My mom could be very talkative and always at the most inopportune times, so of course, she had more to say. "Are you bringing anyone?"

I stopped my pacing. *Like who?* I wondered to myself, feeling impatient as the footsteps drew closer.

"How is your friend Klaire? We haven't seen her in a while. Why don't you bring her along?"

She must have heard my unspoken question. "Yes! I will," I replied immediately.

My mom was either oblivious to the hastiness in my voice or she was intentionally ignoring it. I was betting the latter.

"Good. It would be nice to see her and there will be plenty of food."

I silently chuckled. When wasn't there? She always cooked up a storm.

"Your dad is insisting on making his 'famous' veggie burgers, even though I've told him those things have never been famous at Sunday dinner. Or anywhere else for that matter."

I was suddenly engulfed in a deliciously sweaty body with arms encircling my waist from behind, the solid chest was firm against my back as I felt warm lips pressing into the side of my neck.

"You smell good." Aiden's gruff voice whispered into the ear that didn't have my phone pressed to it.

"Hi." I whispered back, feeling warm and tingly in all the right places.

"Who is that?" My mom asked, more than loud enough for Aiden to hear as he trailed kisses along my neck.

"I...I..." I stuttered when he casually cupped my breasts. I cleared my throat. "Yes. Klaire and I will be at dinner to tomorrow. I'll see you then. Bye Mo–"

"Are you with a man?" she asked, cutting me off.

Aiden chuckled and I groaned.

"He is more than welcome to join if–"

"I'll see you tomorrow Mom, love you." I hit the end button before she could add anything else and turned to face Aiden. "You mister, owe me breakfast."

He took my lips for a hard kiss, squeezing me tighter into his arms. "You're only using me for food, aren't you?"

I resisted the fierce need to climb up his perfectly obessable body. "Among other things."

"I'm going to require some form of payment," he said, biting down on my earlobe.

I moaned and wrapped my arms around his neck, and he took that as his cue to lift me up against his body, my legs circling his waist. I loved it when he did that. "What kind of payment do you have in mind?"

"Why don't we discuss it in the shower?"

I laughed with my face buried in his neck. "Pervert! But, yes please."

CHAPTER 28: CHRIS

"OH GAWD! THIS IS SO GOOD."

My eyes fell shut as I savored the explosion of flavors that danced on my palate. These had to be the most delicious spinach crepes I'd ever had. The thin pancake-like pastry was stuffed with eggs, onions, mushrooms and some other ingredients that made me want to weep in prayer. It was official, Aiden was an amazing cook. I definitely couldn't let whatever it was that we were doing end, if only so he could cook for me. And cooking was just one of the *too many* things he did so well.

Aiden added more sliced fruits to my plate. "I'm glad you like it. One of the joys of cooking is having someone to cook for."

If I were the kind of person that swooned, I'd be doing just that right about now. But since I wasn't, I sighed instead. Did he really just say that? That had to be the most personal admission he'd ever made willingly and it made me smile.

I was internally gloating when he added, "Or so my mom would say to us."

My smile quickly faded as an "Oh" escaped my lips.

Was he saying he personally didn't feel joy in cooking for someone or was he trying to take back the Freudian slip. It certainly wouldn't be the first time he'd let his true feelings slip out. And seeing the calming delight in his expression and our carefree banter when he cooked, I'd bet he enjoyed cooking for others *or* me. I mean, he did make a trip to the grocery store after his workout session this morning so he could prepare breakfast for us. That spoke volumes, didn't it?

But wait a minute.... who's us? His mom would say that to him and his father? I'd hate to put a damper on our lovely breakfast conversation, which had mostly consisted of: work, his trip to Seattle tomorrow afternoon, what we were doing today, and other mundane things as we sat in the kitchen enjoying each other's company, but I had to ask. My list of questions was getting longer and I feared there would never be a good time to get answers. My lips parted to speak, but like a coward, I lifted my mimosa filled flute to my lips, silencing myself as I drained the remnants. Perhaps my subconscious knew I needed the liquid courage.

"Would you like more?" he sounded amused as if in challenge.

I shook my head before shoving pineapple pieces and strawberries into my mouth.

"You're quiet all of a sudden," he commented dubiously. "What's going on up there?"

Well yeah, and it wasn't sudden, by the way. He brought up the mom subject – the same one he got all evasive over last night, I thought to myself rather than saying the words out loud.

"Who is 'us'?" I whispered in a voice that got drowned out by his cell phone, vibrating on the marble countertop.

Aiden's gaze flickered to the screen before reaching to answer it. "Hello."

I looked down at my plate, gathering my thoughts while I polished it off.

"Now is not a good time," he said as he stood, walking down the hall and disappearing around the corner to his home office.

I pushed off my stool to wash the dishes and made quick work of wiping down the counter and stovetop, and put everything back in its place. When Aiden hadn't reappeared, I went up to the bedroom to retrieve my phone before returning to the kitchen. I read text messages Klaire had sent a couple hours ago and was getting ready to give her a call when Aiden rounded the corner.

"Thanks for cleaning up," he said, strolling to the stove area and pulling out two bottles of water from a bottom cabinet.

Deciding to call Klaire later, I placed my phone on the counter. "You're welcome. Thanks for breakfast."

He handed me a bottle without my asking if I wanted one, which I took anyway, then moved to lean against the stovetop across from me.

I studied him as he took a long drink from his bottle, noting the change in his demeanor. He was tense in a way that had the biceps of his free hand flexing involuntarily as his other hand gripped the bottle more tightly than was necessarily. It was like he wished he were drinking something other than water. The loosely fitted t-shirt he wore strained against his chest, giving me a peak at the low-slung waistband of his gray sweats. I uncapped my bottle and took a sip of water as I continued my study of him with a perceptiveness that would've made Sherlock Holmes proud, but it didn't take a detective to know this change was probably as a result of the call he'd taken moments ago.

"Have you decided on what you want to do this afternoon?" He asked.

"Everything you suggested sounds great, so why don't we go with all of the above. You teach me poker, then we test out the new video game, followed by a round of golf at the country club, drinks out on the terrace in the jacuzzi and then spend the rest of the day in bed." I offered, reciting our earlier conversation and hoping for a laugh or at the very least a smile.

He gave me both and appeared to relax. "I think that by the time we've completed three items from that

265

list, there would be no *rest of the day* to spend in bed," he placed his empty bottle on the counter behind him and braced his hands on either side. "So how about we start with that first, since we don't have a lot of time? Which reminds me, Lucas and I will be leaving for Seattle earlier than planned. The Weenor folks are leaving the country on Monday so we had to move our Tuesday meeting to Sunday evening."

That sucked!

The Weenor motion company was looking to do another film adaptation with PGE and after months of scheduling conflicts, PGE and Weenor had finally worked out a date and location for an in-person meeting. The Gamers' conference was ideal since both parties would be attending. On the bright side, the meeting would still be taking place, it just meant less time for us to spend together.

"What time is your flight?" I asked.

"8 a.m., which also means I won't be here for the 11 a.m. furniture delivery. Would you mind being here for that?"

"No. That's fine, I can stay till after the delivery."

He nodded. "Thank you."

"Is that what your call was about?"

He furrowed his brow.

"The meeting." I clarified.

"No. Marge left me a voicemail regarding Weenor."

I nodded, knowing that his assistant often worked weekends just like the rest of us.

"What was the call about?" I asked, going for casual as I drank from my bottle.

If the clenching of his jaw was anything to go by, then I knew I had failed. "It was Isaac."

Well that made sense. His father always seemed to have the power to turn his mood to shit. I just wish I didn't have to witness a lot of it so I didn't have to pry him with questions that I was very sure he would think was none of my business. And rightfully so. "Everything ok?"

He frowned. "Yes. Why wouldn't it be?"

"Geez, I don't know. Maybe because whenever you talk to him or see him," I said, motioning with my hands, "all of a sudden, your mood changes and not in a good way. Like last night for instance, you were rude and dismiss–"

"With good reason," he cut me off, his tone icy, the controlled look on his face telling me to drop it.

My phone sounded, alerting me to a text, but I ignored it.

I took a deep breath, deciding to venture on. "Aiden, I'm going to say something and you may feel I'm overstepping my bounds," I paused, watching him. "Clearly, you and your dad have some unresolved issues, your mom being one of them like you mentioned yesterday. And from what I have seen, he is *trying*. Why not hear him out? How long do you plan on putting him off?"

I took another breath as he stared back at me. His features were now completely devoid of expression. "Don't you want some...peace to feel whole again?" At his almost mocking glare, I noted that that didn't make much sense to me either.

He pushed away from the counter and strode slowly towards me, slipping both hands into his pockets. I strained my neck slightly from the stool I was perched on when he moved to stand directly behind me.

"How about I put a piece of me in your…hole again? Preferably a *different* hole," he whispered softly into my ear.

His words immediately caused goosebumps to scatter all over my body as his breath warmed my skin. I sat immobile, straightening my neck forward and fighting off the sensations stirring within me. He wasn't even touching me, yet I was squeezing my thighs together in need. I knew what he was doing. He was trying to distract me and I refused to let him.

I felt him lean in closer, his lips caressing my ear. "How about it?"

"You didn't answer my question. How about we talk first?" I whispered back, when all I wanted at the moment was for him to take me. We could have our talk much later. Couldn't we?

"We are talking," he countered.

"You have so much anger towards him. Why not talk to him about it?" I guess I did want to have this conversation now after all.

"I'm not angry with him, but that doesn't mean he deserves any of my time."

I made to swivel the stool around so I could see him, but he halted my effort by holding it in place. "But you are, Aiden. The anger permeates the air around you whenever he's present. Anyone can see that."

"You were right," he said.

I looked over my shoulder at him, but he stepped away, clearly wanting to avoid eye contact. "Right about what?"

"Overstepping. I appreciate your concern, but this isn't something you need to worry yourself over."

My gaze followed his movements back to the other side of the counter and I hopped off the stool to follow in pursuit, but stopped myself. "Can you blame me?" I asked impatiently, throwing my hands up. "I have witnessed your interactions and I see what it does to you. You talk in your sleep, for Christ's sake. How can you tell me not to concern myself with any of it? I'm sorry, but I can't pretend. I can't be a robot for you."

"What did you say?"

I stopped my rambling, his frozen eyes and impenetrable countenance giving me pause. "What?" I asked in a whisper.

His expression was chilling. "You've heard me talking in my sleep?"

"Yes, mostly you're apologizing to your...." I paused hesitantly.

"To whom?" He demanded in a voice that was barely audible.

I'd unknowingly taken a few steps closer to him. "Your mom. You're telling your mom you're sorry."

"When? When did you hear this and why haven't you said anything?"

"A few times actually. I'm sorry, I didn't know how to bring it up and when I ask personal questions, you dodge them like a ninja," I finished, exasperated.

"A ninja?" he asked.

"Well, you can be dodgy and evasive at times," I said defensively.

An almost-smile played at his lips. "I assure you, I'm no secret agent."

I loved how he could turn playful despite being epically pissed. "Why do you blame him for her death?"

He was silent for a few seconds before he answered, "Maybe I blame him, but mostly I blame myself?"

"Aiden–" My phone started ringing on the counter, but it barely registered. "You said she died in a car accident. Was your dad driving?"

"No, but we did kill her." He turned away from me to face the kitchen window, staring off for a few minutes. "She'd been battling depression for years, but I took off anyway, not wanting to deal with any of it. I left her in New York to fend for herself so I could go off on self-centered pursuits. When the drinking started, I got her into rehab. I thought she was getting better." He turned back to face me. "I made frequent visits and rehab was going well, but I should have known. *He* should have fucking known."

Blinking rapidly, I willed myself not to cry. He definitely did not need a weeping woman on his hands. "Aiden."

"So yes!" he snarled, "I fucking hate him for that too."

My gaze jerked to the text alert coming from my phone. I had four missed texts and two calls from Klaire. That couldn't be good. When I looked up at Aiden, his hands were fisted in his pockets as he stalked towards me again.

"Aiden–" I beseeched.

"Just so we're clear, this isn't what *this* is."

"What?" I asked, not grasping his meaning.

"This talking, this sharing B.S," he gestured between us, now standing only inches from me. "This is *not* that."

Ok, that kind of stung. We never did discuss what *this* was. "How do you know?"

"Because I don't do this." He clipped out with a dangerous glint in his steely blues as he gripped my upper arms.

I was forced to strain my neck back to meet his gaze, my ire rising as he tightened his hold on me. How did he manage to turn my feelings of sympathy into swirling fury in under a minute? "I wasn't trying to make this anything more or even suggesting that it was." I spat out, trying to loosen his grip.

"Good! Now we can both be crystal," he barked, jerking me closer to him and causing the tie of my robe to come undone, revealing the lacy tank top and black lace panties I wore underneath. "What this is, is fucking! Plain and simple, and I think now is as good a time as any for a reminder."

And I thought now was a good time to cool off. "Why don't you take a minute to calm down?" I suggested, needing a minute to myself as well.

His eyes drifted down to my heaving chest before he released my arms only to pull my top over my chest to expose my breasts and hardening nipples. I twisted then gasped when he anchored me in place, one hand across my back, gripping my butt as the other slid down my stomach and into my panties.

"Aiden," I groaned, pushing at his chest.

"I don't need cooling off. I'm perfectly calm." He leaned in to take a nipple into his mouth as two fingers plunged into my weeping core. "This is what you're here for. This is what you want. Are you going to deny it?"

"Stop," I whimpered weakly. I wanted him, I always wanted him, but not like this. This felt like a punishment and I wasn't sure what I was being punished for. He was torturing me, sucking and squeezing my heavy breasts as I instinctually began to ride his fingers.

He slipped his thumb into my mouth and whispered in my ear. "Stop? Are you denying you want this? Are you denying me your sweet pussy?"

I groaned and bit down on his thumb as I thrashed against him.

"Now you don't want to talk?" he taunted, slipping his thumb away. "You're catching on faster than I'd hoped. No more talking. No more questions. You will offer me your cunt and take my cock whenever I please. Is that clear?"

I was opening my mouth to give him a scathing response when he slid down my body and closed his mouth over my sex. He yanked my panties to the side and squeezed my bottom, sucking vigorously on my clit even as I struggled against the impending explosion. Still too furious at his words, I jerked my hips to dislodge his mouth, but this only enhanced the pleasure that was scrawling down my spine. I braced my hands behind the counter at my back, refusing to give him the satisfaction of having my hands on him. No no no, I mentally chanted as he successfully manipulated my pussy into submission. I clamped a hand over my mouth to stifle my scream when the blinding orgasm hit me with the force of a sledgehammer.

Chapter 29: Chris

When the high abated, I shoved away from him, yanking my top down and panties up as I made for the stairs.

He was hot on my heels. "Where are you going?"

I ignored him and was halfway up the stairs when I felt a pull on my leg and lost my balance. I was swirled around in his embrace, my butt plopping down on the seat of a step with Aiden immediately ceasing the opportunity to wedge himself between my legs.

"What are you doing?" I huffed, shooting daggers at him.

"I wasn't nearly finished with you," he said, pulling at my panties, the angle of my legs impeding his intentions.

"Well, I am!" I spat out. "I guess your *reminder* didn't take."

He looked deathly serious and amused at the same time.

I struggled against him. "Get off."

I heard the ripping of my panties just before he lifted his hips to pull down his sweats. "I plan to once I'm deep inside."

My eyes whipped to his mouthwatering cock as he stretched my thighs further apart and poised it to my entrance. I moaned when he fucked into me.

"*Fuck you,*" I gritted.

Oh gawd! oh gawd! Had it really been mere hours since he was last inside me? It felt like weeks. I beat my fists into his chest and gripped his shirt as he fucked me mercilessly, the heat of his body melting away the cold feel of the steps beneath me.

"*Aiden.*" My voice was hoarse and desperate.

He took my mouth in a hungry kiss, his hand reaching underneath my tank to grope my breast. "You want this, you need this as much as I do."

I ignored his statement of fact and brought his mouth back to mine.

He hoisted my bottom up and pounded away without pause. My fingers moved to claw at his back, wanting and needing more of his punishing strokes.

"You're still so fucking tight." He muttered.

I brought my hands to his face, which was buried in the crook of my neck. "What are you punishing me for?" I whispered.

He tried shaking my hands free, since his were occupied with different parts of my body, but I held on.

"Look at me. Why are you punishing me?"

He slammed harder into me. "Shut up," he gritted. "We're not talking now."

I pressed forward and kissed him with everything I had until my inner walls clenched and convulsed around him. "*Aiden*," I cried.

He pounded in a few more strokes then exploded deep inside me on a loud guttural groan, his thrusts slowing as he collapsed on top of me. My hands roamed over his back, the weight of him soothing me. Moments later, I jolted out of my stupor and shoved at him, remembering the missed calls from Klaire and the fact that I was angry with him. When he lifted himself off, I made haste towards the kitchen to grab my phone and immediately dialed Klaire, but there was no answer. I needed some time away from Aiden and I really needed to get a hold of Klaire.

I made my way back to the stairs, where Aiden was now sitting with his elbows on his knees and his head resting in his hands. Moving past him, I headed straight to the bedroom and quickly changed. I grabbed my things to leave the apartment and was almost out the door when I heard his voice.

He sounded almost pained when he asked, "Where are you going?"

I answered without looking back, afraid I would change my mind and stay. "Not sure, but I need to leave."

"Are you coming back?"

I paused for a moment. "I don't know."

Turning the door knob, I pulled and exited his apartment without saying another word.

Christen and Aiden's story concludes in:

Merger Takeover - To Have

Book II in the Takeover Series

Coming Soon.

About the Author

Alesanda is a free spirit who lives to bring her dreams and imaginings to life through the art of writing. She is an eternal optimist, often drawing inspiration from her travels while exploring the world. She enjoys meaningful togetherness with family and general shenanigans with friends.

Let's Get Social!

Facebook - facebook.com/alesandaelani

Instagram - instagram.com/alesandaelani

Twitter - @alesandaelani

www.ingramcontent.com/pod-product-compliance
Lightning Source LLC
Chambersburg PA
CBHW062132170626
46813CB00002B/673